The Promised Plan

Sharon Hughson

Book Cover by Covers by Kay

Printed in the United States of America

ISBN 978-1-7339342-7-5
Inkspired
11923 SE Sumner Street, Ste. 924294
Portland, OR 97250

Sharon Hughson

In loving memory of my mother
Dedicated to all who grieve

A Promised Plan

The Master Plan

The room tilted, throwing Ruth Glenn against the doorway. She slumped, panting and blinking, against the cool wood while her fingernails dug into the molding.

How she despised the weakness of her flesh.

I have things to do, Lord. Important things.

The dark spots faded, and her stomach stopped flopping like a beached fish. She took a tentative step toward her desk. Before cancer, she managed the post-surgery ward at a prominent hospital. Now she couldn't walk from the kitchen to her bedroom without stopping for a break.

No matter what her body said, she refused to give up. Not when she had formulated a plan to fix the rift between her daughters. She needed to act on it. Today.

My girls need to reconnect, Lord. Because she feared they would need to lean on each other all too soon.

She white-knuckled the back of her office chair, carefully spinning it before collapsing onto its padded seat. She scooted close to her computer, letting her hands manipulate the mouse so she could check the reservation site. Thank the Lord for wheels. Maybe she should use this chair to get around the house.

Except that reminded her too much of a wheelchair and being an invalid. She wouldn't go there. Not as long as her legs could carry her from room to room.

A photo of her and her husband Dale standing by a sign in Mt. Rainier National Park smiled from her computer screen. She loved the Pacific Northwest, had lived there her entire life, and still hadn't seen all its beautiful spots. Likely wouldn't see them.

She clicked the icon for her vacation club, banishing the memory of her travels. Remembering conjured too much pity over everything this disease had taken from her.

Lord willing, there would be time for one more trip.

The club's reservation calendar went out thirteen months. With the girls' busy schedules, she'd need to give them plenty of notice. She selected dates which would hold the condo for twenty-four hours.

Time to make two telephone calls. It would be simple enough to call Lacey. They spoke every Saturday without fail. If she didn't call by ten, Lacey would phone her.

Lacey. Ruth scanned the wall of photographs in front of her. She located the black and white photo of her daughters wearing matching Easter dresses. Her girls. Always so different. Getting Lacey to comb her hair and put on a dress often required threats and bribery, while Krista could sit for hours as someone rolled her hair into curlers.

Ruth's eyes slid shut. She pictured her towheaded girls rushing through the church yard with their Easter baskets, so competitive. Sometimes Krista even beat out her bossy older sister. Their arguments and laughter echoed through the years. No matter how much fighting or fussing or competing they did, the girls always stood together when opposition came.

Except this time.

Her cancer wasn't the cause of their division, was it?

A sigh pressed through her chapped lips. Whatever had driven a wedge between them couldn't be permanent. She would do everything in her power to remove it.

She picked up the land line. Her grandsons assured her such a thing was going the way of the dinosaurs. A chuckle escaped her at the recollection of that conversation. Never a dull moment with those boys.

. After the third ring, Lacey answered, "Good morning, Mom. How are you feeling today?"

Ruth despised that question. In her opinion, only old people seeking sympathy talked about their health woes. These days, everyone asked about her health, while she stubbornly refused to dwell on it.

She sighed. "I'm tired. Merci and I had our shopping trip yesterday."

Since her granddaughter was six, Ruth had taken her shopping for her birthday in July. Sixteen years now.

A brief silence. "You overdid it, didn't you? Merci shouldn't have—"

"I made the appointment. Don't blame your daughter."

"Well, she shouldn't have kept you out all day."

She hadn't. They had gone to exactly three stores and hardly browsed the sales racks as they usually did.

Ruth wished she could return to the days of shopping for hours and watching her granddaughter try on clothes. Now that Merci worked in her favorite clothing boutique, she knew exactly what she wanted and the size she needed.

"We shopped for less than two hours and then spent

nearly that much time having lunch."

"I hope you're taking it easy today."

Ruth's body wasn't giving her another option.

"Enough about me. I called because we came up with a fantastic idea yesterday at lunch."

"Okay." A stretch of silence. "I'd love to hear about it."

"Merci and I were discussing the fun times we have together. And I mentioned one of my favorite places was Victoria, BC, and she hasn't been there."

Two months ago, Ruth had watched Mercedes walk across the stage at her Bible college to be awarded a diploma in psychology, but Ruth had been too sick to take her granddaughter on the graduation trip she'd promised. She really hated breaking a promise. Especially to her grandchildren.

"That's the place with that garden you love."

"Butchart Gardens." Ruth nodded and her lips relaxed into a smile. "And I said it would be great to take a girls' trip there." She swallowed. Darn this dry mouth. "And she thought it would."

Ruth reached for the nearby water bottle, finding it nearly empty. She swooshed the warm, stale water around her mouth.

"A girls' trip."

She hated the robotic tone of her daughter's voice. Lacey had always packed her emotions away, but since she'd left her husband at the first of the year, it had been worse. Exponentially.

Ruth swallowed the water. "You, Merci, me, and Krista."

Lacey's laugh was short and mirthless. "She's too busy with school." And although that reference could have applied to both Merci and Krista, Ruth understood it was a cut at her other daughter.

"This would be after she finished next May."

Lacey's indrawn breath was louder than the rest of the conversation. "That's a year from now, Mom." *You might not be alive.*

Ruth clenched her teeth at the unspoken, but inferred implication. She would not bow to cancer before seeing this through.

"I'm not giving up. That transplant is supposed to get me five good years."

Not that her energy had returned, as the oncologist had promised. More than a year after the stem cell transplant, a procedure that nearly killed her, her bone marrow still couldn't produce healthy blood cells.

"Of course you're not giving up." Lacey sounded offended at the thought. "But a lot can happen in a year."

"Which is why we need to get this on the calendar."

Lacey sighed. "What are you thinking?"

Enthusiasm welled in Ruth as she explained about the condominiums in Victoria. They could drive to Port Angeles and take a ferry across the Sound, so they'd have a car to get to Butchart Gardens. She closed her eyes, envisioning the acres of roses. How she loved roses.

"So, the first week of August?" Lacey sounded interested.

"What do you think?"

"I can plan my classes around it." Lacey had enrolled in a program to earn a nutritionist certification, something that paired well with her personal trainer credentials.

"Won't you be done by then?"

"Maybe. I might have to take fewer classes in the fall if I can't figure out financial aid."

Ruth opened her mouth to offer her daughter the money, and then shut it again. Lacey needed to be independent. Her marriage had destroyed her self-esteem and Ruth believed if her daughter could accomplish this new goal on her own, it would resurrect her confidence.

"Wonderful. I'll make the reservations."

"Don't hold your breath about Krista." Bitterness made her daughter's words bite.

Ruth straightened her spine. The sour tone confirmed that if she was ever to see her girls let go of their feud, this trip needed to happen. Ruth feared their falling out had something to do with Lacey's divorce, but that seemed unlikely since Krista had been advising Lacey to leave the marriage for several years—not that any of them believed in divorce. After Lacey walked out, she had stayed at her sister's home for a month until she found an apartment near her place of employment.

"I don't hold my breath." Ruth sounded as stiff as she felt. "And I don't know why she wouldn't want to come."

Lacey muttered something that Ruth ignored because she worried it would discourage her.

After they said their goodbyes, she trundled into the kitchen with her water bottle. Her mouth tasted like plastic from the stale drink she'd been forced to take.

After she guzzled half a glass of water, she rinsed and refilled her bottle and made a pit stop in the restroom before settling into her desk chair again.

That trip through the house had been easier. Yes, her legs still trembled, but she hadn't been dizzy. Once she finished the second call and made the reservations, she'd lie down for a nap.

She sighed at the thought but refused to berate herself.

The life of a cancer survivor involved multiple daily naps. Even though the constant fatigue drained her, she could keep a positive attitude.

Lord, I'm convinced this trip is what you want. Help me be wise as I deal with this situation.

She dialed her youngest daughter, unsure whether she'd catch her at home since Krista usually attended college classes on Saturdays.

Her son-in-law answered the phone. She loved him. Krista had made a great match with Todd.

"She has class until three. I'll have her call when she gets home," he told her.

They chatted for a few minutes, and, to her delight, he didn't ask how she was feeling. Once she hung up, she made the reservations.

Lord, this is my act of faith. I believe you're going to work it out so my girls can go to Canada and recover their friendship.

She slept through lunch. Dale woke her when he returned from puttering at the parsonage. Since they'd retired, they spent at least one day per week gardening for their church. It had been one activity she'd continued through the first and second rounds of chemo, but now it made her skeleton ache.

He shook her shoulder softly before planting a cool kiss on her cheek. "You didn't eat."

While she roused herself and brushed her short hair, he made lunch. She nibbled at the half sandwich and polished off the bowl of chicken and vegetable soup. Across the narrow table, he sipped a cup of coffee and filled her in on the work progress. After washing the soup pan and loading her dishes into the dishwasher, he headed to the garage to put his tools away.

Back at her desk, she had her computer read scripture aloud while she played several games of Spider Solitaire. Of the many things she'd had to give up, she missed reading and gardening the most. Since she couldn't concentrate well enough to read print, she'd learned to appreciate audio books.

It was close to 3:30 when the phone rang. She picked up the receiver with a brief prayer on her lips.

"Hello."

"Mom, hi. Todd said I missed your call."

Ruth nestled the phone closer. "I thought you might be in class, but I wanted to call while I was thinking about it."

Krista hummed in agreement. "What were you thinking about?"

Well, well. No preliminary questions about her health. Warmth spilled into her stomach, and she chose to accept the immediate interest as a positive omen.

"Merci and I had our annual shopping trip yesterday." She went on to describe it without any interruptions from Krista.

"So, what's this great plan you two cooked up?" She could almost hear the smile in her daughter's voice.

"It involves the four of us girls traveling together."

A brief pause. "Traveling where?"

Lord, give her an open mind. Don't let Lacey be right about this.

After she swallowed a sip of water, she said, "Victoria, BC."

Krista gasped. "I would love to go there. Do you think we could do the high tea you told us about?"

Ruth smiled, cast her eyes heavenward, and relaxed into her chair. "Most definitely. We'll have to have hats for the occasion."

Krista groaned. "Not a hat, Mom. I can't wear hats."

"You most certainly can wear hats."

Ruth's lips twitched at this old argument. Krista wore baseball caps on rare occasions and stocking caps in the winter when weather required it. Otherwise, she hated wearing anything on her head.

"You look fantastic in hats. I look ridiculous."

"Pshaw." Ruth sipped her water. "I'm not going to argue with you about it."

Krista huffed, her sign of capitulation. "I've got class until the middle of August and then a couple weeks off before the next phase of courses begin. I'm finally getting into the student teaching portion." Her joy and energy played in stark contrast to Lacey's lack of enthusiasm. "It looks like I've been approved to work with the language arts teacher at our high school."

"Wonderful news." Ruth cleared a sudden lump in her throat. "This trip is the first week of August next year."

"Next year?" Silence buzzed between them.

"Yes, and you'll be done by then. Graduated, licensed, and employed, I'm sure."

"I hope." Krista sighed. "The first week of August is before the school year starts."

She heard the rumble of a male voice. Krista must have covered the receiver because all went quiet.

Ruth's spotted, wrinkled fingers tapped the water bottle. The sight of her hand reminded her she truly was getting old. But as Dale always said, it was better than the alternative.

When the pain burned through her bones, Ruth didn't agree. Heaven meant the end of pain. But she was adamant that her girls were reconciled first.

"Todd says I should definitely go. And take notes on what he needs to see when we go in a few years."

"Todd's a smart man." Generous. Kind.

Krista grunted playfully. "You always did love him better than me." It was an old joke. Except Ruth didn't think it was funny, especially since she suspected her youngest daughter truly believed her words.

Ruth raised her chin. "I'm not taking him to Victoria, so I think that settles the issue."

After a brief pause, Krista asked, "Lacey agreed to this?"

"Why wouldn't she?"

"And she knows you're inviting me?"

Ruth closed her eyes and relaxed into the headrest of her office chair. A deep ache bloomed in her chest. She would not permit this estrangement. Family stood together.

"Yes. She's excited to see the gardens, and she'll love the tea, too." A wave of fatigue blinded her. Ruth should ask Krista what this disagreement was about, but not today. Not with her body betraying her as if she hadn't taken one nap already.

After a moment, her daughter said in a more subdued tone, "I'm looking forward to it, Mom. This is a great idea."

"I think so, too."

After assuring each other they'd talk at church the next day, Ruth hung up the phone.

If she couldn't get her daughters back together before then, Operation Victoria Girls' Trip would provide ample time and a perfect atmosphere.

She sipped water, gazing over the wall of photographs, recalling the lifetime they represented.

With her mission accomplished for the day, she allowed her mind to rest.

Master Mind

Master mind
      The one behind
      Intervention
      Reconciliation
      Family time

Master mind
      One of a kind
      Determination
      Resolution
      Mother bear

Master mind
      Time to find
      Indelible
      Incredible
      Synchronicity

One rose-filled garden
Two estranged sisters
Three fancy teacups
A plan to keep a promise

The Master's plan

Part One
January

The Last Birthday

Despite the scent of freshly baked cake, an antiseptic hospital odor clung to Grandma's living room. Mercedes Bloom pasted on a bright smile and stepped inside. Life and recent events had taught her the value of faking emotions to suit situations and avoid confrontations.

Relatives clogged the entryway. She slipped in behind her cousin Hunter, bumping him playfully with her hip. He turned solemn chocolate-bar eyes on her, a slight tilt touching the corners of his lips. If she ever got around to making them cousin crew shirts, his would read: "I'm the serious one." He was closest to her in age and had always served as a foil for her off-the-wall suggestions.

"Hey, Merci." She wished she knew what occasion-appropriate silliness she could enact that would bring a real smile to his face.

"I'm here," she chirped and tossed her purse and coat onto the piano bench.

Grandma had volunteered to keep her mom's piano after the divorce last year. With Dad acting like the wronged party, Mom had been fortunate to walk away with a few photo albums and her clothes. Merci had been glad to be removed from the drama since she'd been in college.

But Grandma had put herself in the middle, and Dad hadn't been able to stand up to her. Most people couldn't. Except, now Grandma couldn't even stand up.

Merci's throat constricted and moisture stung her eyes. She squelched the tears and bustled toward the sound of her mother calling, "In here."

In Grandma's U-shaped kitchen, Mom and Aunt Krista stood at opposite ends of the counter, getting things ready for the impromptu birthday celebration. Her mother's shoulders were stiff, and the women worked silently, shouting the fracture in their relationship. Most of the time, conversation buzzed between them.

Merci sidled closer to her mother for the expected hug.

"Glad you could come." Her mother's words ruffled Merci's fine blonde hair, while she held on a few beats longer than normal.

Merci patted between her mother's jutting shoulder blades, wondering if she was eating enough. When had their roles reversed? She knew when, but it wasn't the time to revisit those dark days. Divorce was its own sort of death, and today was supposed to be a celebration of life. Even in the shadow of Grandma's fading health.

"Hey, Aunt K."

Her aunt turned away from the plates she'd been setting out to give Merci a full-frontal hug. Their eyes met as Aunt Krista pulled back, and the tears shimmering in the blue-green pools on her aunt's face reflected the sorrow Merci had squelched during the forty-minute drive from Portland.

Merci's lips flashed their ready smile. She knew no words were necessary since a deaf man would hear the unhappiness in the room. And only part of it came from the impending departure of a woman they all loved.

The front door opened, and her brother Lucas announced his arrival by saying, "Saved the best for last."

Merci shook her head as her younger brother shuffled into the crowded living room, the corner of which was visible from the kitchen. Lucas had shot up in the past few months and stood eye-to-eye with Uncle Todd, who gave him a one-armed hug since he held his camera in the other hand. At a couple inches over six feet, her brother could claim "I'm the tall one" shirt these days but in her eyes, he still deserved "I'm the obnoxious one." The thought made her lips quiver into a small smile.

What would Stephan think of her family? He'd met Mom and Grandma at their graduation ceremony—her bachelor's degree and his master's. Grandma had winked at Merci, later confiding his dark good looks were the type to make girls swoon. What would Grandma say if she knew they were getting more serious?

As Merci returned to the main room, Grandpa Dale wandered aimlessly between the television and the bed. The head of Grandma's hospital bed—the new and unwelcome fixture at the center of the room—was raised, and Merci's youngest cousin Jon stood on its nearest side, holding Grandma's hand and talking animatedly.

As the most sensitive one of the boys, Merci voted Jon most likely to weep through the funeral. Not that she'd be cruel enough to announce that title on a t-shirt. With his dramatic flair, he'd earned the "I'm the funny one" shirt years ago, just as she'd claimed "I'm the talkative one" as her badge of honor.

Merci punched Lucas lightly on the shoulder as she circled the bed. One glimpse of Grandma's pallid face, and she had to swallow down a wave of sadness.

"Grandpa." She threw her arms around him, burying her face in his shoulder, glad for a chance to hide while she corralled her sorrow.

He felt frail in her grip. When had her grandparents grown old?

"How's my favorite girl?"

She inhaled the familiar smell of detergent, fabric softener, and sawdust. The anxiety of the moment ebbed. During her rocky childhood, this home and these hugs had been her haven. After her parents' divorce, she wanted to sink into that safety, but now another earthquake rocked her family's world.

"Busy." She squeezed his arm as she pulled back. "Glad to be here."

He returned the gesture, keeping his palm on her back as she faced the ugly reality of the hospital bed. The white-sheeted monstrosity didn't belong in this room where laughter and family gatherings had ruled.

Grandma had been the center of it all. Now, a tube ran from beneath the sheet and into a bottle beneath the bed. The pink nightgown Merci had bought her the previous Christmas hung from Grandma's bony shoulder.

Pain slugged Merci in the gut. She bit her lip and fought the rush of tears. With a hard blink, she imagined slamming a lid on her unruly emotions. The master's program in counseling she'd started was attempting to teach her how to compartmentalize stressful things until she could deal with them. She'd failed at both compartmentalizing and dealing.

And also at the master's program Grandma asked her about in every conversation. The one that sent Merci to volunteer at a suicide hotline. She closed her eyes and clenched her fists, refusing to think about those dark things. Lord willing, the anxiety those conversations brewed inside her would stay sealed in its box. Today, she needed to focus on being present for Grandma, who had always been there for her.

"Hi, Grandma." She leaned in and kissed the papery skin on her bony cheek, even more lined than it had been when she'd visited three weeks ago.

That had been before the bed arrived. Back when Grandma hadn't given up the fight.

Not that Merci blamed her. Cancer treatments took a toll, and Grandma had been fighting for five years. It was enough to deflate the strongest spirit, derail the hardiest faith, and defeat the most determined fighter.

"Merci." Grandma's rough lips scraped against her cheek. "I need to talk to you."

"I'm right here."

Before Grandma could say anything else, Mom came to the head of the bed. Her smile looked forced as she glanced around at everyone.

"We're all here, so let's sing the birthday song—"

"And dive into the cake," Lucas said, proving how well the "obnoxious" shirt would fit.

Jon elbowed him. Good. Merci would have done it if she stood within reach. Lucas should know that his booming voice needed to be toned down for this party.

Grandma's last birthday didn't sound like much to celebrate.

Aunt Krista nudged in beside Mom and started the song, her alto voice ringing clearly. One by one, the boys joined in, but Merci had to swallow a huge lump before adding her clear soprano to the mix. Thankfully, Aunt Krista had started the song a bit low. Even with the boulder of emotion in her throat, it wasn't a stretch to hit the high notes.

"There's cake and drinks in the kitchen," her aunt said and hurried that way, throwing herself into role of hostess.

Clearly Merci wasn't the only one avoiding facing feelings head-on.

Mom reached over the mattress and squeezed Grandma's shoulder.

"Do you want a piece of birthday cake? Yellow with chocolate frosting."

Grandma hadn't eaten much chocolate in the past several years. When she'd been on chemotherapy, it didn't agree with her stomach. Then her oncologist had put her on a strict anti-cancer diet, restricting her sugar intake to nothing.

No need to worry about that anymore.

"A sliver." Grandma held up her thumb and index finger with barely a space between them.

Grandpa patted Merci's elbow as he passed her and did the same to Grandma's feet beneath the blanket. He met Uncle Todd near the dining table, and they headed toward the kitchen.

Predictable. An offer of cake cleared the room of hungry men, making it ideal for a private moment with her grandmother.

"Closer." Grandma fumbled with the bed controls.

Together they raised the head a few inches, leaving Grandma nearly upright. Merci leaned in, lips trembling into a smile. Grandma would see through it. No one saw as much as Grandma did with those icy gray eyes, and there would be no hiding Merci's breaking heart behind a cool facade.

"I need you to promise," Grandma said and smacked her chapped lips. She'd struggled with a dry mouth even before cancer came calling, but now it was worse.

Merci retrieved a plastic cup from the nearby rolling table and held the straw in front of Grandma.

Grandma took a small sip. Swallowed. Everything slowed. Merci memorized the way the light from the kitchen cast a halo above Grandma's silver pixie haircut. The way compassion added a hint of blue to her eyes.

After returning the cup to the table, Merci wrapped her hands around Grandma's.

Grandma's gaze pierced Merci's. "You have to promise to take the trip."

Merci blinked. Her muddled brain spun, processing her grandmother's request. The trip. Her dying grandmother wanted a promise about the trip to Vancouver Island?

"Your mom and Krista." Grandma swallowed hard. "They must take the trip. Together."

Over the past eight or nine months, Merci had watched her mother withdraw from life. The bubble she'd created had room for work and family. At least, everyone in the family except for Aunt Krista. Since her aunt was finishing her master's degree and had hours of student teaching to complete every week, the combined family time they'd shared for many years had dwindled to holidays.

But best friends made time for each other. Their close ties had always prompted Merci to consider her cousins like additional brothers.

"Grandma—"

Skeletal fingers dug into the back of Merci's hand, and she nearly flinched.

"You have to carry out our plan—" Grandma coughed lightly— "after I'm gone."

The words sucker-punched Merci's heart. She couldn't draw a breath. Agony twisted through her chest and up her throat.

She tightened her grip on Grandma's hand and leaned closer, catching a glimpse of her mother weaving through the crowd of bantering boys. She'd arrive with the cake in seconds.

"I promise," Merci whispered into Grandma's ear. "We will go to Victoria BC in August." What else could she say? At the best of times, she couldn't deny her grandmother, so in this moment she didn't even consider a denial.

She kissed the sallow cheek again, drinking in the scent of tea tree shampoo and the hint of flowers from the sheets. She squeezed her eyes closed, imprinting the moment in her memory.

"I brought your cake," her mother chirped, not fooling anyone with her false cheer.

"Thank you."

Grandma shared another meaningful look with Merci before she fumbled with the paper plate holding a sliver of cake.

As Merci took her slice of cake from Mom, doubts about her ability to keep the promise stole her appetite.

No one matched the unstoppable force of Grandma.

But the baton had been passed. Overwhelmed and honored, Merci silently committed to making the trip they'd previously discussed happen. To seeing Grandma's faith in reconciliation between her aunt and mother become a reality.

Merci hoped and prayed she could handle the challenge.

For Grandma. Merci straightened and tuned in to the familiar family chatter. She sliced the cake with her fork.

Lord help her, she would find a way to fulfill Grandma's final request.

The Day God Answered a Prayer

Krista White imagined an ugly gremlin clawing its way through her gut, burning her throat like acid reflux. She hugged her chest and rooted her feet to the laminate flooring of her parents' living room. Here, a short—and seemingly endless—four days earlier, the family sang happy birthday to her mother.

Mom had been alert. She'd nibbled cake and talked to everyone. Today, she hadn't even sipped water.

On the opposite side of the hospital bed, her sister Lacey leaned over their mother. The withered body under the sheets mocked Krista's memories. Where was the dynamic and determined woman who often provoked her with mountainous expectations?

"I'll be back soon, Mom," her sister said, peachy lips an inch from Mom's ear. "I love you."

After she planted a kiss on the pasty, wrinkled cheek,

Lacey's eyes brushed over Krista, not staying long enough for Krista to lock gazes. The silent communication they'd practiced for decades hadn't been used in months.

"You'll stay while I'm gone?" The accusation was clear. During the past three weeks, while their mother lay dying, Krista had been absent too often.

Krista nodded. She didn't trust the knot of emotions to stay in her stomach. As much as it pained her to admit, Lacey was correct. Krista was guilty of abandoning this sinking ship.

She knew they needed to talk about the rift in their relationship, but this wasn't the time or place. But would it ever be the right moment to cross the frozen tundra separating them? Opportunity hadn't presented itself. Both of them worked and Krista was busy attending graduate school to get her teaching certificate. She would finish soon. Maybe then she'd have energy for that confrontation.

Or maybe not. Not when more baggage would come with Mom's passing.

Dad reached up to hug Lacey from the leather rocker he'd pulled close to the bed. The living room that once boasted two sofas and matching recliners had been invaded by palliative care paraphernalia.

Because cancer was winning. The woman who had fought hard and overcame many obstacles during her seventy years of life couldn't defeat lymphoma.

Emotion choked Krista, deafening her to whatever words passed between her sister and father.

At the door, Lacey turned and stabbed Krista with her signature big sister glare.

"Call me if anything changes."

Krista ducked her chin, glancing toward their father who

wilted into the chair a few feet away. Let her sister take that as an affirmative. She hadn't cornered the market on emotional trauma. Krista was losing her mom, too, even if she'd always felt like Lacey and Mom shared a closer connection.

The door closed. Silence descended, louder than a ticking clock.

"Can I get you anything, Dad?" she asked after swallowing the lump of sadness.

He shook his head. "Thanks for being here. I know you're busy."

Guilt stabbed. "I'm not too busy to be here for you, Dad."

Wednesdays were days when missing her student teaching didn't create a gap. The teacher she worked with had given her the rest of the week off anyway. She'd affirmed that Krista was doing a great job and a few days off wouldn't set her back. According to her mentor, her family needed Krista more than the students.

As gratifying as approval from the veteran English teacher felt, Krista preferred the structure of going to work each day. Time in the classroom helped her avoid the skydiving plummet of impending loss.

Her mother was dying. How could she face that?

"Lean into Jesus," her best friend from church said. Krista was trying. Truly. If she leaned into him any harder, they'd become the same person.

Her mother drew a breath. It rattled in her chest.

Krista stepped closer, frowning at the otherwise immobile form. In life, her mother never stayed this still. Another wrench of her gut brought physical pain, and Krista crossed her arms over her middle.

Earlier in the day, the home health nurse had stopped by to check on Mom. Krista had asked about the labored breathing. After listening to Mom's lungs, the woman assured them they were clear. She was as fine as could be expected.

The breathing sounded painful, and Krista's chest ached with sympathy.

Mom hadn't spoken to them since before the nurse's visit. In the past couple of hours, she hadn't opened her eyes. Since she wasn't eating or drinking, it was clear her time on Earth was short.

Krista bit her lip. She paced a few steps and stared out the picture window.

On the sidewalk, a woman walked her poodle. Across the street, the neighbor's garage door opened. Life continued. That reality complicated the grieving process. Krista's heart said the world should stop turning until she could catch her breath. Until she was ready to stop crying.

But the sun rose and set. People laughed and lived. Ready or not, life went on.

So did her mother's raspy breathing. Krista paced the floor, finally escaping around the corner into the kitchen. She filled a glass with water from the refrigerator door and sipped it while staring out the window over the sink.

Mom's garden plot was covered in mulch. Winter ravaged the plants, so Lacey had pulled everything out in November during one of Mom's hospital stays.

She'd been in and out of the hospital since late September, needing platelet transfusions every three weeks, then every two. When she waited too long, her heart rate bottomed out and she ended up back in the hospital.

Now there was a Do Not Resuscitate order attached to

her file. Krista knew it well.

Three weeks ago, Krista had taken her mom in for a routine doctor's appointment, and he had admitted her. Every nurse that walked into the hospital room needed to confirm that the DNR was correct.

How many times did a daughter have to repeat that her mother was dying and wanted to be allowed to go? Too many. Krista couldn't get away from there fast enough once Dad had finally arrived.

That reaction painted her as a bad daughter, and probably increased her sister's ire.

After swallowing more water, Krista paced toward her parents. Dad's head slumped to the side. He hadn't been sleeping well, even though Lacey had been staying with them since Friday, trying to relieve the caregiving burden. Dad had been responsible for it since the cancer struck five years before, only two years after Mom retired from the nursing career she'd loved and excelled in.

Krista leaned against the bed, humming a hymn. Her mother loved to hear her sing, but during the past week, it had been difficult to do. Watching a strong woman fade away certainly wreaked havoc on a daughter's heart and stole her desire to praise God. If one more person told her she was lucky to have this time with her mom, she might scream.

There was nothing lucky about being on the sidelines at a deathbed. Last week, family and friends had stopped by, a regular parade of well-wishers, reminiscing and doling out hugs. Mom smiled and laughed. But that time had passed. Now, she was too weak to get out of bed.

Another breath ground out of her slightly parted lips.

Please, Lord. Don't let her suffer.

Krista smoothed Mom's short, white hair away from her forehead. She felt cool and didn't respond to the touch. Yesterday, that contact would have set eyelids fluttering, giving Krista a brief glance at her gray eyes.

She swallowed another batch of tears and walked around Dad's chair to stare out the window. Not that she saw anything. Laboring breaths filled the room. The sound grated against her nerves.

A tear slid down her cheek. She slashed it away.

Please, God. Just take her. She would hate being like this.

Her mother had always worked hard, managing five or six activities at once. Rather than sitting idle, her hands clacked knitting needles together or organized a box of photos while she watched television beside Dad. This total lack of movement pained Krista nearly as much as the harsh sound of breathing.

How could Dad sleep? Each breath cracked like thunder.

Krista fidgeted but stayed by the window. Sunshine flared from behind gray clouds, a rare break in the Oregon rain. Those rays empowered her to maintain a grip on sanity. Winter was the worst season. After this, it would be a constant reminder of death.

Please, God.

But that was all the prayer she could muster. The last few days, her prayers had been short and desperate. Every night when she arrived home after stopping to check on her parents and tell Mom she loved her in case it was the last time, she fell against Todd's chest and wept. How could there be more tears inside her?

Without Todd, she would have drowned in grief. And Mom wasn't gone yet. How would Krista survive the actual passing?

More cacophonous breaths rattled through the room.

She paced the hallway, trying to escape the ominous sound. Photographs of her boys and her sister's kids lined the first wall. Family photos were around the corner. In Mom's office, the walls were plastered with framed pictures, black and white to color. Only the wall beside the window had none because that's where the overloaded bookcase reigned.

Krista's eyes scanned the familiar scenes, not seeing or remembering. Just trying to dodge the present.

She wandered back into the living room. Dad slept. Mom's breath gurgled.

Krista stood in front of the window again, pleading for the horror to end. It hollowed out her soul.

Clouds covered the sun, and Krista shivered. She hugged herself more tightly, rubbing her upper arms. Maybe winter would never end, and the ice field of her heart would keep her flesh frozen.

A sudden silence pounded in her ears.

She turned toward the hospital bed. Mom remained unmoving. Completely still. The horrendous dissonance of breaths had stopped.

Krista's heart plunged into her gut. Trepidation slowed her shuffling steps to the bed. She rested a hand on Mom's shoulder.

"Mom?"

She gently shook her. No flickering eyelids or twitching mouth.

Krista bent down to place her cheek in front of her mother's slightly parted lips.

"Mom?"

Not a wisp of breath. The silence she'd prayed for had

come.

No. Please.

"Dad, I think Mom's gone." Her voice pitched with desperation.

Her father jerked awake and stumbled to his feet, disoriented for an instant.

"Ruth?" He shook Mom gently, repeating her name several times.

A torrent of tears slicked Krista's face. The scene of her father imploring her mother to wake up blurred and seemed to shrink.

"She's gone." Dad's voice broke.

Krista rounded the bed and wrapped her arms around him. His shoulders seemed diminished as they quaked beneath her cheek. For a long time, they stayed together, sharing their agony with gulping sobs.

"Should I call someone?" Dad sounded lost.

Krista stiffened. She needed to let Lacey know.

The ball of emotion choked her again. If she tried to say the words, her tears would strangle her, cutting them off. Todd would understand. She'd start with him.

As Dad shuffled to the kitchen phone, Krista retrieved her cell phone from her purse. She pressed her husband's number. He answered after two rings.

"She's gone." A sob ripped the final word in half. She could not do this. She could not tell everyone that Mom was dead.

"I'll be there as soon as I can." His voice was steady. Todd, her rock. He couldn't get there fast enough.

He said more that her brain didn't register. After she ended the call, she brought up her sister's number. Her finger hovered there. Lacey needed to know; she deserved to hear the news immediately. Krista's hands trembled. Finally, she pushed the message bubble instead of the call icon.

She would regret that decision later. It wasn't the way Lacey should learn about this monumental loss. But in that moment, typing the words could have been climbing Mt. Everest. Krista's lungs didn't have the capacity to say what her quivering fingers typed: *She's gone.*

Dad's voice droned, sounding a bit stronger as time clicked forward. Krista clutched the chair at the end of the dining table where her mother often sat. In her vacant heart something strange rushed to fill the void.

A flood of emotion pooled there, rising and expanding. It soothed and filled the cracks of anguish.

Krista closed her eyes. When she identified the strange sensation, more tears surged. Her heart welcomed the new feeling even as her mind rebelled.

Relief.

On its heels came a tidal wave of guilt.

She had prayed for this. God had granted her wish. And now she had the audacity to feel relieved that her mother was dead?

Here was ultimate proof that Krista was a horrible daughter.

Once Upon a Funeral

January won the award for worst month of the year. After last year's horrible first month, Lacey Bloom didn't think she could hate the month more passionately.

Lesson learned. Never call out the universe.

A niggle somewhere in the icy plains of her heart whispered that once upon a time she'd believed God controlled the universe. She crushed the reminder. The woman who had believed in a divine Creator who lovingly cared for his children ceased to exist when said God didn't heal her mother.

During the past year, she'd hovered on the edge of giving up on God when "Christians" exponentially increased the pain of her divorce. After all the years she'd given serving in her church, the pastor had believed the worst about her, and her other so-called friends stopped returning her calls a few months after she'd left her husband. If their judgmental actions and abandonment exemplified God, she wasn't missing anything. Even though it meant facing the loss of her mother alone.

A desire to weep surged upward from her chest. She clamped down on the urge. There was no way she would give those people the satisfaction of seeing how they'd broken her.

The last song of the service swelled and ended, one final haunting note hanging in the air. Dad, silent tears wetting his cheeks, pulled Lacey closer under his arm. He needed her to be strong, and she wouldn't let him down.

Not like her sister had let her down. The firestorm Lacey fueled with resentment bubbled below her aching heart. But now wasn't the time for those thoughts or emotions.

Sniffles and sighs filled the brief silence as the pastor made his way behind the pulpit. Lacey glanced toward her daughter who gripped Dad's hand, tears leaking down her rosy cheeks. Pride flooded over the ache in her chest as she studied talented Mercedes whose college degree guaranteed her a host of life options. At the very least, her daughter would never have to depend on a man to support her.

On Lacey's other side, her son's jaw worked. While the pastor announced the reception line and church-hosted dinner, Lacey patted Lucas on the thigh. He leaned toward her, gaze fixed on the photograph of Mom at the front of the sanctuary. Facing such a loss while still in high school seemed unfathomable. Especially since Lucas was caught in the middle of her divorce debris, and Lacey hated that.

Was it better to see his mother belittled daily? Did he understand how controlling his father had been? What husband gave a woman a monthly budget of $250 and expected that to cover groceries, school supplies, and gas to run her teenager to his practices and events? The same sort of husband who threw a fit when his wife took a part-time job to earn the money required to take care of her children's needs.

Leaving a marriage that sucked the life from her meant leaving her son to endure his father's clutches alone. An emotional soup churned in her gut and sent a wave of nausea through her.

People moving around her as the pastor invited them to stand jerked her from the fruitless musing. Once upon a time she would have looked forward to seeing old friends and family. Not today. Socialization meant coming face-to-face with some of her former friends, and her nausea increased at the thought. After sitting through this funeral, her heart couldn't withstand additional pain.

And if God existed, she would have asked him to spare her and her children the ordeal.

But since he had taken her godly mother, why would he care anything about her? Someone with a heart as jaded as hers would never find mercy from him anyway. She wondered why she'd ever believed in him when the past year had proved him non-existent.

She squeezed her dad's hand as the pastor led in prayer, not hearing his droning words. Together, they walked out of the pew and down the aisle. Her sniffling sister fell in behind them, her emotional outburst competing with the ongoing prayer. Lacey imagined Krista wrapped in her husband's comforting arms. Fiery antagonism stewed, stirred by Krista's thoughtless actions during the weeks of hospice and especially the day Mom passed.

Krista hugged Lacey's arm before ducking into the restroom. Lacey flinched at the contact. Last year, they would have sought solace together and faced the string of grievers as a united front.

Once upon a time, they would have leaned on each other. A shared look would convey their dread of this emotionally draining procession. Sisters of flesh and mind, they understood what words never conveyed. Except Krista had chosen a college degree over family responsibilities. A knife slashed across a heart Lacey believed numb from loss.

She slammed a door on the onslaught. Facing hard things alone seemed to be the theme of her new reality. And she dreaded facing the line of people to come. Because their hugs and positive thoughts wouldn't change the facts.

Her mother was dead. Words failed to breach the gulf created at her departure. Even the fact she was in Heaven wasn't a positive spin. Not when Lacey felt uncertain that Heaven was real since God didn't seem to be. She knew Mom believed, and today that would be enough assurance for her. But while Mom might be in a better place, Lacey still had to learn how to live without her wisdom, encouragement, and unconditional love.

Once Krista returned, Dad embraced his girls. "I love you. Your mom was so proud of you."

Krista's teary cheeks pressed close enough Lacey smelled the vanilla from her sister's favorite shower gel. Lacey's heavy chest echoed like a dark cavern. Feverish tears filled her eyes and nearly escaped the prison of her eyelids.

But, no, she would be tough. For Dad. For her kids. She blinked hard and squelched the welling sob. Holding up would make Mom even prouder.

Dad's grip tightened on her shoulder. She wanted to bury her face in his dark jacket. Before her heavy limbs complied with her wish, he pivoted toward the sanctuary's open doors, a man at the mercy of a firing squad.

People clad in dark-colored clothing filed into the

vestibule.

The horror show of the day marched on. Right now, she needed to survive this cultural ritual. Somehow. Once she didn't have an audience, she'd weep over the loss of her mother's constant, loving support.

Emotion choked her. Grief stung her eyes. She banished mourning's side effects with the force of her will. Mom had taught her how to persevere over debilitating emotions. She'd employed those lessons daily for the past year. She would continue living by them because what other choice did she have?

Friends of her mother's passed by and shook her hand. Mutters of, "What a lovely service," and "Your mom was amazing, she'll be missed" blended together. Empty words. Meaningless prattle. She painted on a smile and nodded to each person.

When someone hugged her, she stiffened. She didn't want to be comforted or assured of God's love. Since she'd decided God didn't exist, he couldn't be mad that she nursed her anger at his unfairness. Accusations swelling toward her sister wanted acknowledgment. A pit of rage overflowed within her, and she welcomed it because it thawed the ice of grief.

Still, she smiled, nodded, and murmured appropriate responses to the trite platitudes. Until she saw the next people in line were her former pastor and his wife, the Danes.

She bristled, and churning acid in her belly bubbled over, burning from stomach to throat. For four years, she had worked side by side with this couple, as a teacher and leader of the children's outreach ministry. But when she needed their support, they'd failed her. Worse, they'd taken Grant, her ex-husband's, side and believed his false accusations. Their betrayal made Judas' kiss seem friendly.

Anna Dane reached to hug her. Lacey shuffled back a step. The powdery sweetness of the woman's perfume suffocated her as hot, moist hands patted her shoulders.

"Your mama was a blessing to all of us." Her slight southern drawl reminded Lacey of her favorite aunt, and she almost relaxed into the warmth of the woman's bosom. "I know she wanted to see you back in church."

Those words formed a metal rod in Lacey's spine. How dare this woman presume to speak for Mom! Lacey and her mother had talked about the church situation numerous times. In fact, Mom had expressed disappointment that this woman made assumptions without talking directly to Lacey. What sort of pastor's wife encouraged people to judge and shun someone?

Lacey's mom knew the truth. Although Lacey had tried to sugar-coat it, she'd relayed some examples of the mental abuse Grant rained on her for years. Regardless of her general beliefs about the sanctity of marriage, Mom had agreed Lacey shouldn't be punished for breaking free from such a damaging relationship.

But the Danes? They'd let Grant's lies that her correspondence with another man was proof of an affair sway them. What employee didn't email their boss? The messages Grant had retrieved had been complaints against him and consolation from her boss. Nothing more. Still, this woman chose to believe the worst and side with a man who rarely attended church.

As she jerked free of the embrace, Lacey glared into the woman's hazel eyes. Anna shook her head, and her gentle smile turned upside down. But the disapproval rolled like water from a duck's back. Lacey knew Anna only talked like a Christian but didn't love "sinners" the way Jesus had.

The woman had barely moved past before Pastor Duane took her place. He shook Lacey's hand without meeting her eyes.

"Praying for you, sister." *To repent before God chastises you.*

She completed his prayer in her mind. His prayers didn't matter because she didn't believe in them. Hadn't everyone in this building prayed for Mom's healing? Prayer served no purpose that Lacey could see.

Prayer was useless because she didn't believe in a God whose people afflicted the wounded. Not only did he allow her loving and hard-working Christian mother to suffer and die, but he permitted cruel so-called Christians to continue thriving. Where was the justice in that?

The line of people blurred. She shook hands or returned hugs but couldn't recall faces. A familiar high-pitched voice jerked her from the protective stupor. It was her long-time friend, Gwen, who didn't know the meaning of using an indoor voice.

Lacey gripped the skirt of her black dress. When Gwen had gotten a divorce, Lacey had offered free childcare so she could attend college. Over the years, Lacey had given and given, including this friend in her children's life. Their friendship had thrived to the extent Merci and Lucas called her Aunt Gwen.

She'd seen Grant's destructive moods firsthand. With wide eyes, she'd watched as he belittled the kids and called Lacey stupid and useless. While she'd worked to keep the house spotless and grow and preserve the vegetables he didn't consider part of her monthly allowance, he'd criticized everything from the way she dressed to how the kids didn't keep their rooms tidy enough.

But when Lacey needed a supporter, Gwen had caved to popular opinion. Within a month of the divorce, Gwen's calls and visits stopped. Everyone from church shunned Lacey, including this woman who had been a second sister.

How fitting that neither her real sister nor her soul sister would fight for her. Only her parents remained stalwart. And now Mom was gone, and Dad was fading into a shadow without her.

Gwen crushed Lacey with a hug. Moisture pressed against her chin from Gwen's teary face. Lacey couldn't relax into what should have been a comforting embrace. It was as false as the friendship she'd known for two decades.

"I'm picturing her in God's garden." Gwen sniffled and dabbed her face with a crumpled tissue. "She'll be happy there."

Mom had been happy here with her children and grandchildren. She'd been needed and loved here. Why did people believe a statement like this comforted someone in mourning? The stew pot of incendiary wrath churned through Lacey's chest.

Gwen patted her back. "We should get together soon. I miss talking sewing with you."

Sewing? Lacey hadn't sewed a stitch since she walked away from her marriage. The well-supplied sewing room had been left behind. Her controlling ex had forbidden her to retrieve anything she didn't take the night she "abandoned" him. Being free of his dominance and negativity meant more to her than those lost possessions.

Mom had known some things needed rescuing. She had managed to retrieve a few framed pictures and two photo albums, along with the piano. But only because no one denied her once she'd set her mind to something.

Grief swelled from the hollow pit in Lacey's chest, strangling her. She coughed and swallowed it back, nodding to Gwen whose tremulous smile meant as much as her empty words.

Gwen still had her mother. She couldn't possibly fathom the depths of darkness drowning Lacey's soul. And her lack of contact in the past nine months proved she didn't truly care. Even though Gwen had resurfaced the final month of Mom's life and took up residence in her parents' living room, humming and reading Bible passages out loud. Like she'd been there all along.

"Okay," Lacey choked out since Gwen held her arms hostage.

After another quick embrace, Gwen moved on to hug Krista, whose face was streaked with moisture although she made no sound.

Regret pinched in Lacey's chest. She hated watching her sister cry. But no one could take the source of pain away. Mom was gone. At least Krista had been at her side when it happened.

Bitterness rankled, raising Lacey's pulse. She had asked her sister to call with updates. Could she do that? Nope. She'd sent a text instead. *She's gone*, it read.

Who did something like that? Didn't such an announcement merit a phone call? Even if Krista had sobbed her way through the telling, Lacey deserved to learn the news from the lips of someone who loved Mom. Not read impersonal words on a screen.

Ire battered Lacey's compassion for her sister. Besides, Krista had plenty of support from the church people streaming past. She hadn't been cast out. She hadn't lost everything.

Lacey had no one. No friends. No church. A broken family. And no mother to lean on for advice and reassurance.

Dad's arm slipped around her shoulders. She started before melting into his side. Her father had been a lifeline during the past year. Now, the roles reversed. Lacey needed to be resilient for him.

"That's the last of them." He patted her upper arm. "I'm stepping out for some air before heading to the dinner." She doubted he'd eat much if his stomach was as knotted as hers.

Lacey opened her mouth to say she'd join him. Her children slipped through the sanctuary doors, banging into each other's sides as they came. Lucas looked like a shell-shocked war survivor while Merci wore a forced smile, tear stains and bloodshot eyes telling the true story.

"Can I get you a plate, Mom?" Merci took the arm that wasn't pressed into Dad's side.

"I wonder if Aunt Jane brought her famous chicken and dumplings," Lucas said.

Dad patted her back and relinquished his spot to Lacey's son.

Today, she had her children at her side. She raised her chin.

For them, she could face a fiery furnace. She'd been doing it for years and not even this catastrophic loss could alter her mothering instincts.

"I'm going to catch up with Vanessa." Lacey tried to sound upbeat. It was sad when funerals became family reunions, but Lacey knew her cousin's droll comments would make her smile. Even if nothing could remove the bullet holes in her heart and soul.

With a child on each arm, she headed toward the door. As she passed, Todd pulled Krista into a hug. Their sons circled behind her, creating a cocoon for her sister.

Lacey ground her teeth. Krista had everything—husband, family, friends. Lacey had nothing but this moment with her children before they returned to their lives.

And left her alone. Again.

Meet You At The Gate

A beautiful garden now stands alone,
missing the one who nurtured it but now she is gone.
Her flowers still bloom, and the sun it still shines
But the rain is like teardrops for the ones left behind.
The weeds lay waiting to take the garden's beauty away
but the beautiful memories of its keeper
are in our hearts to stay.
She loved every flower even some that were weeds
So much love she would plant with each little seed.
But just like her flowers she was part of God's plan,
so when it was her time He reached down His hand.
He looked through the garden searching for the best,
that's when He found Ruth it was her time to rest.
It was hard for those who loved her to just let her go,
But God had a spot in His garden
that needed a gentle soul.
When you start missing Ruth, remember, if you just wait,
when God has a spot in His garden,
she'll meet you at the gate.

Written by Barbara Bailey
c. July 2007

https://www.familyfriendpoems.com/poem/meet-you-at-
the-gate

Part Two
July

A Wish and a Prayer

Summer's warm weather and relaxed pace usually infused Krista White with happiness. But this year regret dogged her thoughts and dreams. She'd sought forgiveness for praying for her mother's death and feeling relieved when God answered her prayer. But months later, joy and success remained elusive, confirming her actions that day had brought a curse of sorts down on her.

This call with yet another school administrator proved it.

"I understand," Krista said into the telephone. But she didn't. Not even a little bit. "Thank you for personally letting me know."

The vice-principal of the school where she wouldn't be working gave some final words of encouragement and the call ended. Krista hugged the phone to her chest.

Lord, how many times do I have to say I'm sorry?

She hadn't really wanted the job at a school district in a neighboring town. Not when it meant she'd have a twenty-five-minute commute every morning. Additionally, the position meant teaching seventh grade humanities rather than high school language arts.

"It's a good thing." She straightened her shoulders and replaced the phone in its charging base. Maybe even a God thing.

Her stomach ached and a bitter taste coated her tongue as her physical reaction contradicted the words. She had sacrificed time with her dying mother to stay on track with her teaching program.

If she didn't get a job, that was a resounding pronouncement that she'd made the wrong choice. Her sister thought she had. Several friends at church had also disapproved when she continued her student teaching during the final weeks of Mom's life.

What could she have done for her mother? Nothing. The pastor's wife and a certified nursing assistant from the congregation had taken over daily care until those final days when Lacey stayed with their parents. Unlike her sister, Krista wasn't a natural caregiver.

If that made her a bad daughter, what else was new?

She shuffled to the refrigerator and pulled out butter and eggs. With this latest round of disappointing news, she needed cookie therapy. Both her boys were home from college and would make short work of the sweets. She ignored the niggling reminder of her recent upgrade to elastic waistband shorts.

The stand mixer whipped butter and sugar together, a familiar sight that pushed away her disillusionment. With the blender on its lowest setting, she added an egg, watching the pale concoction fluff and lighten. When she dumped in the vanilla, the sweet fragrance sent a shiver of delight into her sunken stomach.

Her cell phone rang. She flipped off the mixer, smiling a bit at the photo of her dad that flashed on the screen. His grin stretched across his face as he held a basketball overhead. She recalled the day it was taken. He'd pulled up to their house, hopped out of his truck, and snatched the ball from the boys who'd been in the middle of some sort of shooting match.

The photo dated back to her sons' high school days. She blinked, wondering when she'd last seen that smile on Dad's face.

"Hi, Dad," she said.

"Hey, kitten. How are you today?"

"I've been better." She explained about the latest rejection.

"When the right job comes along, God will make sure you get it."

A lump cut off her air. Dad hadn't been angry because she hadn't offered to help care for Mom, a duty he'd embraced as part of his marriage vows. He'd recounted times when Mom cared for him, saying it was his turn to support her. After all, he was retired while the girls had jobs and families.

If he hadn't expected her to give up her dream, why did it feel like God had?

She cleared her throat. "I hope so." He had always been the supportive parent. What had she done to support him since Mom died? The question slashed her aching heart.

Maybe the reason she wasn't getting her dream job had more to do with not learning her lesson than her emotions at the deathbed. She'd sacrificed time with Mom and had somehow pushed her sister away because she'd prioritized getting her master's degree. Was she still putting her desires above relationships?

"I got an email from the timeshare people."

She wrinkled her brow. What did the timeshare have to do with her?

"I need to cancel the unit in Victoria by next week." A long pause. "If you girls aren't going."

Victoria. The girls' trip her mother had planned with zest last summer. In her application and interview rush, Krista had forgotten about it. Was that more proof her priorities were out of whack?

"That's not really my decision." She couldn't imagine spending a week with her sister since they hardly talked these days. When they did, the conversation was stilted and usually focused on how Dad was managing on his own.

"Your mom wanted to take that trip so bad." He sounded wistful. "She'd been trying for years to organize something with her three girls."

Censure plagued Krista's heart. The familiar twinge was an unwelcome reminder of her shortcomings and she sighed. "I remember. But I doubt Lacey will want to go without Mom."

"Your sister needs a break."

She stiffened. Was he blaming Krista for the problems between the sisters? She didn't really understand what started Lacey's grudge.

"You both do." He heaved a sigh. "It's been a rough year all around."

A frog leapt into her throat. She cleared it to say, "Do you want to go? I know it was a special place for you and Mom." Her voice nearly broke on the last word.

After a pause, his sad voice said, "That wasn't your

mom's plan. She wanted you girls to share an experience that she loved."

Except they couldn't share it with her now, so what was the point? In Krista's wildest imaginings, she didn't see a scenario where Lacey would willingly step away from her multiple jobs to spend a week with Krista.

"She planned to pay for the tea. I'll book it as she intended." Dad's voice thickened.

Krista's heart flopped like a caught trout. Since Mom's starry-eyed description of it, Krista had dreamed of taking high tea at the Empress Hotel. Victoria had amazing gardens, and she knew the beauty would be spectacular, but that didn't appeal to her like dressing up and having a proper tea. Weird, since she didn't drink tea.

"I was looking forward to high tea."

"Oh, you girls will love it. My only complaint was the little samples. They need to be doubled in size."

Dad and his sweet tooth. Krista's lips tilted upward. Maybe the trip would be a good thing. It would give her an opportunity to talk things out with Lacey. They'd be together and her sister wouldn't be able to simply hang up the phone. With Merci there, her sister wouldn't want to cause a scene.

"If you can convince Lacey to go, I'm in."

Another pause. "What's going on with you girls? Your mom worried about it."

Her nose tingled. She blinked the sudden wash of tears and sucked in a deep breath.

"I wish I knew, Dad. She's been distant since her divorce, but that doesn't make sense to me. Todd and I were her biggest supporters through that mess." And it had been a giant disaster involving a swarm of false accusations started by Krista's ex-brother-in-law. The fallout devastated Lacey, forcing her out of her church.

But Krista and Todd had offered her a place to stay until she found something across the river in Washington, one closer to her place of employment. Once Lacey moved out, she'd seemed to move on. Krista had tried to stay in touch, but working full-time, attending school, and staying faithful to her women's ministry and teenage teaching positions at church had filled her time and zapped her energy.

After a few months, their texts had become short and their phone calls infrequent. When Lacey claimed she was too busy to meet for lunch that summer— had it been a year now? —Krista didn't push. She'd allowed her best friend to walk away to a life barren of support, except what their parents provided.

"The divorce." He harrumphed. "She spent a lot more time with your mom, too."

Krista bristled. Another accusation? Everyone knew Lacey and Mom shared a deeper relationship and that had never bothered Krista before. Because of their closeness, Lacey had been heartbroken she wasn't there when Mom died, and Krista wished she could have been anywhere else.

"They had a lot of common interests." She was proud of how even her voice sounded.

"I just mean, she's lost an awful lot in the past couple years."

"I get it." Of course Mom's death would be harder on Lacey, but that didn't mean Krista hadn't suffered. She wouldn't have survived without Todd. Thinking of his support made her wonder who Lacey leaned into during the dark times of loss.

Shards of reproach slashed Krista's soul. She'd failed as

a sister and a daughter. Now she was failing to land her dream career. Why should God bless someone so selfish?

Ice stabbed her heart. Her head spun. She couldn't catch her breath.

Dad's soothing tone talked her off the ledge of a panic attack. "I love you girls, but your mom wanted this trip." He paused. "She planned to sit you two down and make you work things out. You could still do that."

Could she? Without Mom to mediate and orchestrate? Krista doubted it.

She sighed. "I'd love to go, Dad. But I can't convince Lacey to agree." The truth of that weighed more heavily than her other failures. Once upon a time, they'd shared every aspect of their lives. As their children had aged and grew more active, they'd had to work harder to find time together, but it had been a priority.

Dad huffed, his signature move when he was losing an argument with one of the women in his life. The heaving shoulders accompanied a hang dog expression, the epitome of a wounded, misunderstood man. Picturing it almost lightened her mood.

"I'll see what I can do."

If anyone could convince her sister, it would be Dad. Since Mom's death, they had become closer than ever before.

"I'm sorry." For so much she could never explain to anyone.

"Don't be." He chuckled. "I have a trick or two up my sleeve."

She shook her head, smirking along with him. "Can I motivate you with peanut butter chocolate chip cookies?"

He moaned. She laughed. "We'll drop some by later."

"I never turn down baked goods."

The conversation ended on a high note, but the niggling sense that Krista had once again failed to live up to expectations remained. Mom had expected her to make things right with her sister. Dad expected her to miraculously convince Lacey to take the trip.

She couldn't manage any of it. Not even getting a job she was highly qualified and certified to do.

Lord, I know I don't deserve anything. But Mom wanted this trip.

She started the mixer and slowly added the dry ingredients. Emotion pressed her head and heart, making it hard to breathe, and the thought of indulging in her favorite treat lost appeal.

Floundering in her whirlpool of self-condemnation, Krista jerked when arms wrapped around her waist. But her pulse revved, when she realized it was her husband pressing his lips to the top of her shoulder.

She flipped the mixer off and turned into his embrace. With her nose pressed against his soft polo shirt, she inhaled the spicy scent of his cologne and savored the warmth of love that melted the ice forming over her soul.

"How was your day?" she asked, peering up at him.

Todd dropped a quick kiss on her lips. "The usual. Yours?"

The comfort of his embrace cooled at the thought of her recent phone calls. She related the latest in her job search.

He squeezed her hip. "The right one hasn't come along yet. When it does, you'll get it."

Confidence swam in his chocolate syrup gaze. How could he believe in her after all her mistakes?

She forced her lips into a smile, wanting to be reassured by his faith in her. With her pulse playing bongos in her gut, she condensed the call from her dad.

Todd nodded. "I'm glad you're going to take the trip. It's time for you to talk it out with your sister."

Her stomach flopped. She knew he was right, and she wanted to have her best friend back. But how many mistakes would she have to own in the name of restoration? The thought of telling Lacey about her prayer...Krista gulped.

Todd climbed the stairs, and Krista powered up the mixer, adding the final cup of flour. The warring factions of hope and guilt pummeled her emotional landscape. Wasn't it time for a truce? Could she wave the white flag and surrender her secret relief over Mom's death?

God, I promise if you get Lacey to Canada, I'll make sure we talk things out. Like Mom wanted.

A sigh of acceptance relaxed her shoulders. Surely, that prayer would make it past the ceiling. Why would a loving God answer a prayer for death and ignore a prayer for reconciliation?

If he answered this time, she wouldn't squander the opportunity.

After all, she owed it to her mother. She might have failed miserably before, but if given the chance, she could grant her mother's final wish.

A Promise to Keep

Without Grandma and their annual shopping trip, Mercedes Bloom's birthday had lost its magic. Or maybe the ticking time bomb of her unkept promise to Grandma was the anchor drowning her joy.

She woke, remembering their final shared look, certain she had dreamed about that birthday party again. Her hasty agreement to the promise haunted her at work, too.

Merci adored Your Plus One, where she'd worked on the sales floor for the past two years. At eighteen, she'd had her thyroid removed and nearly doubled in size. Thankfully, Merci discovered the boutique with fashionable attire for full-figured gals.

Now that she wasn't attending college, Merci worked full-time at the store located in a huge mall fifteen minutes from her apartment. With a smile, she circulated around a display she'd helped set up, offering friendly assistance to two shoppers browsing the sales rack. They selected items which she carried to the changing rooms.

Her favorite part of the job was recommending clothing

and chiming in with compliments when customers donned the new outfits. Merci kept her input honest and kind. The store had styles to flatter everyone, and her sales numbers said the customers agreed.

The day after her birthday, a man called her name. She glanced up from returning clothes to the sales rack.

"Grandpa!"

Her heart rejoiced at the sound of his voice. She left the mass of garments hanging and rushed to hug him. His haggard cheeks covered in whiskers scratched her face.

His eyes carried the same light of love that had guided her heart for a lifetime. "How's my favorite girl?"

Honestly, she was missing Grandma like he was, but she said, "Surprised to see you here."

"Came for the knife sale on the lower level." A smile twitched his mustache. "Thought I'd see if you were working."

It felt like she was always working. Besides the two managers, she was the only full-time employee.

"It's nice to see you." She glanced toward the clock behind the register, ignoring the clerk who hovered there, pretending to straighten items on the hold rack. "I get a break in about twenty minutes."

"Maybe I can buy you a drink."

"A strawberry smoothie from Smooth It?" She donned the pleading expression that had always served as a blank check with Grandpa.

"You got it." This time the smile sparkled in his green eyes.

Closer to thirty minutes later, Merci joined Grandpa on a bench outside the store. He handed her the Smooth It cup, and she slurped the melting drink thirstily. She swirled the straw through the dark pink slush, and he cleared his throat.

The man had a mission. This wasn't an accidental trip to see her. The sudden knot in her stomach confirmed what he planned to talk about.

"I got an email from the timeshare place."

Her heart plummeted to the floor. Sometimes it didn't pay to be intuitive.

"If you girls aren't going to Victoria, I need to cancel."

Cancel? No, they couldn't. Her chest squeezed her lungs, and she stared into her cup. Merci had promised Grandma that the three of them would take the trip. It was up to her to convince her mom and aunt to travel to Canada. Which meant she had to go, too. She cringed at the thought of living in close quarters with them. That would make keeping her secrets nearly impossible.

She raised her chin and met Grandpa's gaze. "We're going. I promised Grandma."

His eyes glistened. He turned his head, pretending to watch an unruly group of teenage boys on the level below.

"Are you sure? I talked to your mom last night. She didn't sound very excited."

These days, her mom didn't sound excited about anything. She worked and went to class and worked out and studied and kept their monthly family game nights. She never stopped moving and hardly ate enough to keep a canary alive. Mom was treading water in the sea of loss, and Merci didn't know how to keep her afloat.

She barely kept her own head above the rising tide of grief. With the three of them together, a tsunami would seem small when compared to their collective pain.

"She'll go. So will Aunt K." They had to. She'd promised.

He nodded. "I talked to her yesterday, too. She agreed to go if your mom would."

His assurance melted some of the tension from Merci's shoulders. She leaned into his side, both comforted and offering comfort.

Aunt K probably needed a break from the grueling work and school schedule she'd been keeping for the past three years. Clearly, Mom needed one from her no-frills life. The trip was Grandma's brainchild, a neutral place with time focused on healing the rift between her daughters.

Merci straightened. "I'll talk to them, Grandpa. We're going."

"It meant a lot to your grandma. This trip." His Adam's apple bobbed in his bewhiskered neck. He'd never left his face unshaven when Grandma was alive. Tears tickled Merci's throat, but she swallowed them along with her slushy drink.

"It means a lot to me, too." Well, keeping the promise did. Keeping secrets? Not as much. "Don't cancel the reservations."

Somehow, she would convince these women she loved to go on a trip she dreaded. And if they resisted too much, she'd play the guilt card. She'd inform them that Grandpa would lose thousands of club points if they didn't keep the reservation. That was the truth even if Grandpa didn't seem to care about forfeiting those points. He wanted the trip to happen because Grandma had spent hours in her last months organizing the details. Merci knew the plan's importance because Grandma had used their last conversation to speak of it.

After work, Merci sat with her bowl of soup and grilled cheese sandwich. At nearly eight, it was late for dinner, but she couldn't fall asleep with an empty stomach.

She set her phone in its stand, perfect placement for the video call she planned to have with Stephan later. Since Grandma had passed, she missed him more than ever. But in the wake of his mother's stroke, his family needed him. She understood the weight of those expectations more than the average girl.

She slurped a spoonful of navy bean soup and glanced at the clutter around her. The studio apartment had been perfect when she'd moved off campus her junior year. She could walk to class in fair weather. Her landlords were members of the church she'd attended since starting college five years ago and blessed college students with a lower-than-average rent.

College students. She wasn't one, and her landlord was one more person who needed to know it. Her mom would flip when she learned Merci quit the master's program she'd been enrolled in via one course per term since graduating the previous summer.

First the suicide hot line and then the internship at the local middle school had dashed every plan she'd made. She wasn't cut out for the job the program qualified her to do. The pain of the girl wanting to take the bottle of pills to end a cycle of abuse had given her nightmares for a month. Learning firsthand about an "uncle" who touched in ways he shouldn't from a seventh grader had broken her. She couldn't even finish the afternoon with the school counselor because her tears refused to be banished.

All of it had happened within months of Grandma's death, and maybe that had exacerbated the roiling emotions. But Merci couldn't spend years and thousands of dollars with a building dread that she would never escape these sorts of horrors.

If counseling wasn't her path, what was? Stephan wanted to explore their relationship.

Her heart flopped at the thought. But he was in California, and she lived and worked in Oregon.

She finished her dinner and cleaned up the small kitchenette—no room to leave dishes out here. She whispered a prayer for wisdom. How would she keep her word to Grandpa?

The video chat signal chimed from her phone. Her heart raced. She dried her hands and pushed the button to accept the call.

Dark hair and eyes shimmered into view. Her breath caught as his olive-toned, square-chinned face filled the screen. A grin stretched her lips, and she settled into a chair.

Their friendship had been strong from the beginning. He'd been a sophomore studying theology when she'd dropped into the youth program he led at church. A large percentage of college students attended that fellowship. It hadn't taken long for Merci to befriend several teenage girls who admired her enthusiastic singing.

Within three weeks, he had asked her to co-lead worship during the teen service. Their voices had blended well as they praised the Lord from the heart. Singing with Stephan elevated her joy in a way singing as a child at her home church never had.

He'd been two-thirds of the way done with his master's program when his mother suffered a severe stroke. It had been six months since he'd returned to California to help his father run their floor covering business. Strangely, their connection had deepened once they began to text and talk more frequently.

"Hey." His smile made it difficult for her to breathe. "How was your day?"

He listened as she related the latest, including Grandpa's request about the trip. Stephan already knew about the promise to Grandma.

"I know you don't really want to go. That's probably my fault."

She shook her head. Of course, Stephan would try to take the blame, but Merci wasn't keeping her secrets because of Stephan's recent invitation. She did it because she didn't think her mom could handle another change in her life.

"I promised Grandma. Now I've done the same with Grandpa."

Lord, why couldn't Grandma have lived long enough to take this trip? She wanted to bring the sisters together, and she would know how to do it.

"You could tell your mom to take the trip in your grandma's honor."

Merci pursed her lips. "We are planning to go where she wanted. And Mom was excited about the gardens."

Stephan nodded and smiled. "Talk about what your grandmother would have loved. That will take the spotlight off you."

And all her secrets. "I wish I could take you along."

"I'm always in your pocket or purse." He waggled his bushy eyebrows. An unruly portion of his slicked back hair flopped onto his forehead.

"Not the same."

"That's why I want you to—"

"I'm thinking it over." She blinked. As much as her feelings for Stephan had evolved from their few months of casual dating in the fall to something so much more now, she didn't know what to tell him.

"I'm not pressuring you. I'm ready for the next step." He leaned closer to the screen until all she could see were his expressive brown eyes. "I love you, Merse."

The thudding of her heart in her ears was deafening. He had been her rock through the grief and changes, regardless of the physical distance between them.

"It feels like running away."

He leaned back. "I see it as running toward your future."

Something settled inside her, like a lock clicking. He was right; he was her future. But before she could move ahead, she had promises to keep. Whatever it took, she would convince her mother to take this trip.

After a pause, she said, "I see some gardens and a fancy tea in my future."

His grin returned. "That's the spirit. If this is the Lord's will, he'll make a way."

Trust the music minister to share a platitude she'd heard most of her life. "I did some research. Some of this stuff is pretty spendy."

Thanks to her dad's stingy control, money had been tight for her mom. He paid no support even though they'd been married more than twenty years, and Mom had stayed at home with Lucas and Merci for most of that time. Merci wanted to be angry at her dad for being selfish but how could she pick a side?

Even though her mom wasn't happy, Merci knew she felt freer. Her parents had been miserable together. Dad wanted to control everything. If he knew Merci wasn't going to college, he'd pressure her to move home. She didn't want to consider what he'd think of Stephan's idea.

"I thought your grandparents had that timeshare."

"The room's paid for. Grandpa said he paid for the tea, too." Tea at the Empress Hotel was nearly $100 per person, so it was a good thing Merci didn't have to fork over cash for that.

Merci recoiled at the thought of the fancy tea. Grandma's seat would literally be empty. It would be impossible not to notice her absence. Merci ground her teeth together and cast misty eyes heavenward. Why had she promised Grandma they would take this trip?

"I could Venmo—"

She held up her hand. "It's going to be fine, thanks. I have to convince Mom to go before I worry about that anyway."

"Sunday is your monthly game night. You can wait for a perfect opening, then hit her with the sad-eyed stare."

Merci leaned toward her phone, donning the expression he spoke of.

"What do you want? I'll do anything for you." He laughed but his gaze was serious.

Her throat closed. She needed him. Why was she putting off a decision?

"You're easy to convince."

"For you, yes." He swallowed. "Your mother loves you, so she'll be easy to convince, too."

Merci doubted it, but she was determined to do it anyway.

Sunday came sooner than Merci expected. After church services, she jumped in her well-used Taurus and drove over the Glen Jackson Bridge. During the hour-long drive to Castle Rock in Washington, she cranked worship songs and intermittently begged God to soften Mom toward the idea of the trip.

The small duplex in an older neighborhood worked for her mother who didn't seem to be home too often. Merci parked on the quiet street, noticing the absence of her brother's rusty blue pickup. Big shock. She'd arrived first.

She walked up the cracked walkway, fanning herself as sunshine scorched her bare arms. After knocking twice on the door, she pushed her way through, calling out a greeting.

The standard chitchat was interrupted by a text from Lucas.

"He needs to finish a paper," Mom said.

Merci whipped out her phone and texted him a scathing message even though his absence meant more opportunity to have the necessary conversation with Mom.

Mom walked down the short hallway to retrieve games. Merci pulled a glass from the plain cupboard and noticed a flyer from their old church on a stack of other mailers.

Merci bristled. The people in that church had been a second family to her during her teen years, but after the divorce, she hadn't talked to any of them. They'd cut off her mother, and that had been an earthquake for Merci's personal faith. No one expected church people to dump a faithful member like a plague carrier while embracing a man who hardly attended services.

No kid wanted their parents to split, but Merci wasn't blind. Her parents had never spent time together, both choosing to fill their free time with separate hobbies and interests. Still, she'd expected the church family to rally behind her mother who taught a class and headed up several committees. Their opposite reaction had shocked her to the core.

The afternoon stretched. Frivolous conversation and joking about the games they played together, cards and

Scrabble. Eventually, they stopped so Mom could make their dinner.

It was time.

I'm keeping my promise to you, Grandma.

Merci mentally crossed her fingers that it was true.

"This is my favorite day of the month," Mom said, pulling salad fixings from the small, shabby fridge. "How is your class going?"

Merci cringed. Topic number one she wanted to avoid, so of course Mom brought it up first. "Grandpa stopped by the mall this week."

"He looks terrible, doesn't he?" Her mother sounded sad.

"He asked about the reservation for Victoria." Merci sucked down a deep breath. "He wondered if we're still going."

Lord, open Mom's heart so I can keep my word to Grandma.

"He mentioned it to me, too." She chopped vegetables vigorously. "I'm slammed with work, and I need to get my coaching plan organized before I start school in September."

"You need a break, Mom. All you do is work."

"And go to school." She sighed. "I've got to pay the bills."

Merci knew all about that. She nibbled the inside of her lip. What to say now?

Help!

"And I can't really afford it anyway," her mom said, tearing lettuce and tossing it on the two plates.

"It's paid for." Merci brought out her cajoling tone. "Grandpa's even paying for the tea."

"He told you that?"

She nodded. "And that Aunt K wants the three of us to go."

Silence greeted the mention of her aunt. Merci's neck flushed. In Merci's memories, her mom and aunt were inseparable. Whatever had happened between them couldn't erase a lifetime of shared experiences and friendship. Could it? She wouldn't let it.

"Not that she has to worry about money." Mom's bitterness made Merci cringe.

Was their fight over money? That didn't make sense, did it?

"Mom, most of the trip's paid for."

Her mother sighed and motioned toward the silverware drawer. "I can't afford a week off."

Merci huffed, setting a fork and knife in front of each chair at the circular vinyl table in an alcove by a window. "It's what Grandma wanted. We need to honor her last wishes."

A weighted silence stretched between them. Mom chopped and Merci refilled their water glasses, sitting them beside the silverware.

Mom might not want to be reminded that the trip was Grandma's idea. But it was. And Mom had been as excited as Grandma about it. Until it became clear that Grandma wouldn't survive to take it with them.

Merci swallowed tears that threatened at the thought of disappointing Grandma.

"I know this trip was important to your grandmother."

A tidal wave of emotion slammed Merci. "Is. It is important. She would want us to go."

She stared blankly out the window. Although she'd helped Grandma come up with this plan, Merci had her own reasons for avoiding it. Would she be able to keep her secrets while sequestered with her aunt and mother?

"I know." Her mom's voice softened.

"She'll be there in spirit, Mom." Merci stepped closer, studying her mother's profile.

Mom cleared her throat. "I don't think I can get the time off. But I'll check into it."

Merci's lips quirked in victory. Her mom's boss would give her the time off.

They talked about her mother's nutrition classes and her plans once she got the certification, which paired perfectly with her personal training job.

As Merci gave a final hug on her way out the door, she said, "Don't forget to ask for that week off, Mom."

"Nag, nag." But Mom's lips curled up slightly, the closest she ever came to smiling these days.

As soon as she arrived back at her apartment, Merci searched for the Holmes Gym website. She copied the email address for the owner into a new email message.

Hey Evan,

I'm sure Mom already asked for this week in August off, and she really needs to take this trip.

Please, please, please give her time off. It's really important to me that we go to Vancouver Island like Grandma planned.

After including a few more pleading sentences, she hit the send button.

Yes, she would beg a man she barely knew if it meant granting Grandma's final wish.

Warmth seeped into the cracks around her heart. She'd done it. Merci had convinced her mother to travel to Victoria as Grandma wanted. And if Mom went, Aunt Krista would go, too.

Step one was done.

Grandma would be smiling down on her. Merci tilted her face toward the ceiling and smiled back.

The Unwanted Vacation

The sunrise bloodied the horizon. Instead of a new day of hope, despair darkened each morning for Lacey Bloom. If she'd believed God existed or cared, he would make the sky cry instead of lightening with summer's glow.

Had it only been seven months since Mom's death? Lacey hadn't wanted her mother to suffer at cancer's mercy, but she relied on her warmth and wisdom. Especially since the divorce left her friendless.

The stoplight turned green. Her second-hand Kia grunted as she pushed on the gas. The past week, it had acted strangely. Just her luck that it would conk out only a few months before she paid it off. The car was her most valuable worldly possession, and it wasn't worth much.

She should have listened to Mom's advice two decades ago, before she married Grant. But she'd been swept up in love. The man knew how to romance a girl until she was caught in his web. During the last ten years, her stupidity had cost her in confidence and contentment. Even now he strove to rob any chance she might have for happiness. But she'd show him. She'd show all of her so-called friends and the not-so-loving church people who'd believed Grant's lies about her having an affair.

If they knew her, they would understand she lived to help her children succeed. A major reason she left the marriage had been because watching their father destroy her also ruined Lucas and Mercedes.

She pulled into the parking lot of the Holmes Gym. A yearning for time in the outdoor pool pushed against her heavy thoughts. If she hurried, she could swim laps before teaching her first exercise class of the day. Since the pool didn't open to the public until ten, she'd have it to herself.

Then she needed to talk to her boss. He would put an end to her daughter's ridiculous notion of traveling to Canada next month. Mom had planned that trip and without her, it held zero appeal for Lacey.

Grief twanged through her scarred heart. To banish it, she focused on the other reason she would never take the trip. Her sister. If they shared close quarters for a week, Lacey would surely explode, and she didn't want her daughter caught in the fallout.

She released the seatbelt and grabbed her bag from the passenger seat. Evan's white truck and another pickup were the only vehicles in the lot.

Her employee badge unlocked the front door, and she marched inside, sparing a brief glance at the unmanned check-in counter before heading toward the office. A message board affixed to the closed door served her well as she jotted a note asking Evan to meet with her at seven.

She strolled across the lobby toward the women's locker room. Weights clanked. Country music blared, drifting from the free-weight room on the lower level beside the three racquetball courts. The murmur of male voices underscored a pause between lifting repetitions. Evan. Her boss had become a friend during her transition to single life.

She didn't have many friends these days.

And if she was to believe the "friends" who had left her behind, being friendly with her single boss invited the ugly accusations her husband made. Was it her fault Evan was the only person who listened to her rants about Grant's controlling ways? Her failed marriage had taught her that too many churchgoers wanted to believe the worst about people. How did that line up with what Lacey read in the Bible?

Lacey pushed the dreary thoughts away with more force than she used to shove into the locker room. After donning her suit, she ducked into a warm shower before heading outside.

A bird chirped a warning as she opened the gate to the pool area and the swim therapy she needed. She inhaled the familiar scent of chlorine and chemicals while adjusting her goggles. Happy memories of team camaraderie and friendly but fierce competition connected her to a fragrance others found offensive.

Her toes gripped the rough edge of the pool before she sprang into the sweet haven with a shallow dive. She swam the length of the pool submerged. Silence pressed against her ears even through the earplugs she wore. Her shadow— long, slender, steady—floated over the turquoise bottom of the pool.

The rhythm of her strokes pulled her into a meditative state. Some people swore by yoga, but swimming was the only thing that lulled her into tranquility. Especially these days when she had no mother or sister to act as a sounding board. In the pool, things like late notices and rising gas prices didn't exist.

She switched from freestyle to breaststroke, her favorite and the one she'd competed in during high school. Water's silky fingers massaged her skin, while consistent inhales and exhales transported her to a stress-free state of mind. Where no troubles existed. Where her life overflowed with friends, church, and a close-knit family.

At the next wall turn, she transitioned to butterfly. One lap of that challenging stroke made her shoulders and lumbar ache. She flipped onto her back at the turn and shifted to backstroke. The sky stretched above, a canvas of possibilities. Summer had always been her favorite season, and in the pool that became true again, no matter how broken her life had become.

She pushed off the wall, twisting onto her stomach to end with breaststroke, swimming until her lungs screamed for a break.

Lacey panted, arms trembling as she pulled herself from the pool. Wrapped in a towel, she trudged in the direction of the gate, in no hurry to return to the real world.

As Lacey entered the dressing room, another woman clad in a sports bra and bike shorts exited. They exchanged greetings.

Lacey rinsed away the chlorine and donned a lightweight tank top and capri-length leggings. A glance at the clock over the doorway showed it was nearly time to meet with Evan.

Weights clashing and televisions blaring from the main exercise room became the soundtrack for her trip across the lobby. The whir of treadmills added a hypnotic undertone.

She pushed open the door her boss always left ajar, closing it enough to dampen the background noise.

At her entrance, he looked up and stood. A massive beast of a desk held neat piles of folders and paper. Evan smiled and gestured to the sofa pushed against the wall beneath his framed diplomas and photographs of his various Taekwondo competitions. He was an eighth-degree black belt, and she'd often seen him working through his forms during her three years in his employment.

"How was the pool?"

"Perfect."

With head nods, they acknowledged a compatriot spirit of people addicted to physical exercise. Lacey claimed one end of the brown leather couch. He handed her a bottle of water from a small refrigerator before settling onto the other end, angling himself to maintain eye contact during their discussion.

"I assume this is about your vacation request for the first week of August." He laced his fingers over his abdomen.

His certainty jolted her. She twisted off the bottle cap and sipped, letting the cold neutralize the sudden wrench in her gut. A warning signal she chose to override.

"The vacation I'm not going to take."

She had penciled the vacation request onto the calendar last year. Back when her mom was alive and talking endlessly about the Butchart Gardens in Victoria, BC.

At the time, Lacey had been thrilled about visiting one of her mother's favorite vacation spots. She'd heard enough from Mom about the roses—a love affair they shared—that she'd wanted to experience them firsthand. Even if it meant staying in her parent's condo with Krista.

Mom had been the mastermind of the adventure. And

Lacey had agreed to it because she didn't want to disappoint her mother, who she knew would serve as a buffer between the sisters. A whisper of emotion tugged at her heart, sadness that once-close sisters needed an intermediary.

"Why not? This is the trip your mom planned last year, right?"

She nodded.

Evan raised his bushy eyebrows. "The same trip you gushed about for months?"

She ground her teeth. "A trip with my mother and daughter." An exercise in endurance with her sister. And she had no energy to spare for that battle.

"I think you should go."

Her heart plunged into her stomach. "Why? I have exercise classes scheduled."

He waved a hand. "I've already asked Tammy to cover them. The vacation has been on the calendar for a year."

"I can't afford to miss work." If her car had its say, she would need to find an extra source of income.

"You have vacation time you've never used."

She narrowed her eyes. This was meant to be a gentle exit from the vacation. He was supposed to be thrilled he wouldn't have to pay for a substitute instructor. In short— he was her alibi, her rock-solid excuse to avoid disappointing her daughter while escaping an emotional volcano in the form of missing her mother and facing off with her sister.

"Most of my money comes from my personal training sessions. That won't be covered."

He frowned. "Maybe we can book those clients for the week after you return."

Her pulse thrummed at her throat, her mouth so dry she

couldn't swallow. "I...That might work." She gripped her palms together in her lap. "Except I'm not going. I've already decided."

He glanced toward the computer on his desk, shoulders hunching slightly. "Merci emailed me."

The conversation barreled off course at high speed.

She gaped. "My daughter emailed you? Why?"

He ducked his chin, piercing her with a knowing gaze. "She wanted to make sure you had the time off. Apparently, she promised your mom you'd all go. Merci wants to honor her with this trip."

Anxiety surged from a deep pit beneath a mental barrier Lacey had constructed months ago. It had helped her survive so many disappointments. She'd needed a bomb shelter for her heart since the text that their mom was gone pinged her phone. Her sister's text. Another slam in a line of shirking behavior that had begun about the same time people from church started drawing away from Lacey.

Who told someone news like that by text? Thinking of her sister's failure energized her reluctance, but she didn't want to air that dirty laundry here.

She gulped water, hoping it contained a miracle solution. "I don't want to go." A tremor entered her voice. And she despised the weakness it implied.

His lips pressed together into a sad smile. "Why not? Too many memories of your mom?"

Tears stung at his gentle tone. She widened her eyes and forced the moisture away.

"It's pointless. It was supposed to be a trip with my mom." She swallowed a bubble of anger. "Since she's not here, why go?"

"Because your daughter wants you to." His words sent a

dart into her chest. "Her email said the plans are all set. If you back out now, your dad loses a deposit."

She covered her nose and mouth, sucking in a deep breath. It didn't help. She hated that Dad would lose the timeshare credits. But that didn't mean she had to go and confront constant reminders of her loss. Not when it would strain her non-existent finances.

Facing off with her sister would cause the elephant in the room to stampede. Lacey would not trap herself where Krista might try to make amends. Too much was unsaid and unresolved between them. Krista had failed to show up when Lacey needed her. Because she was too busy living her perfect life and avoiding the hard things.

"They can take the trip without me." Although she knew that wouldn't satisfy her daughter. Why did she have to suffer because of some promise her daughter made? "Merci and I can do something else." Something with fewer relationship grenades.

"What is this really about?" He cocked his head.

Maybe she could make him understand. Maybe he would even agree with her logic. The reins on her bottled grievances loosened.

"I can't stand the thought of being with my sister. She hardly carried any of the weight during Mom's final days." Her heart pounded. "Then wept through the funeral and cleaning out Mom's closet and jewelry box." Lacey bit off the words. A bitter taste coated her tongue.

"Everyone grieves differently."

"I know. But she could have helped me." *And stood up for me with the church people.*

But the biggest resentment came during Mom's final hours. That last afternoon, Krista had stayed with their parents while Lacey ran errands. It was payday, and she'd needed to get to the bank so she could pay rent.

She closed her eyes, ignoring the ache of missing her mother's final moments. Lacey had been the main caregiver, and she should have been there. Instead, her sister—who had avoided being alone with Mom—got that privilege. And then whined about how hard it was to hear those final breaths.

Fury burned away the ache of loss. Lacey swallowed and opened her eyes.

Evan stared at her. For so many months, he'd been her only confidante, but for some reason she didn't want to voice her list of grievances against Krista. Not even to him.

Was it because she knew it was overblown?

She squelched the niggling doubt and stood, suddenly wanting to move, pace, do something.

He sighed. "Your mom wanted you and your sister on this trip together. Why do you think that was?"

"To make a memory. And if she was there, it would be fine." Not great, for sure. And knowing Mom, she'd try to have some intervention for them, making them talk it out as she'd done when they were teenagers.

But it would have been okay. Mom would have made certain it played out equitably. Even if there were raised voices and tears, Mom's steady presence would have mediated. Lacey might have been okay to work things through with Krista that way. But not without Mom.

The knot returned to her throat. Evan didn't understand, and he wasn't going to be the safe zone she needed. Not today.

He stood, facing her with concern reflecting from his eyes. "I hope you'll reconsider. I told Merci that you were good-to-go as far as work was concerned."

Of course he did. Because nothing could be easy. Most people wanted to go on vacation, and she would rather do anything else. Even if Mom had believed it would be a bonding experience, and Evan believed it would help her through the grieving process. But Lacey hated to disappoint her daughter who had suffered so much already.

"I'll let you know later today."

She bolted from the room, needing a reprieve from emotions—one she would find in exercise class.

Clearly, she was being forced to face this problem head-on. She wouldn't be the cause of her daughter breaking any promises. Wasn't her broken promise to love, honor, and cherish the girl's father hard enough for Merci to live through? She wouldn't want the guilt she fought to become a resident in her precious daughter's heart and mind.

Lacey jogged down the steps into the gymnasium. She doubted anything good could come from this trip. Not without her mother captaining the ship.

More likely, Lacey's lifeboat would capsize, drowning her in the sea of broken dreams.

She raised her chin. Good thing she was a strong swimmer.

Stages of Grief

Denial
>This isn't happening
>God would never take her
>She loves him and loves us
>Her life is meaningful
>The doctor must be wrong
>Treatment can be a cure
>Think about something else

Cancer, I hate you.

Bargaining
>God, let her live
>I'll do anything
>Take me instead
>We need her here
>Our family's heart
>If you love me…
>She deserves healing

Creator, I beg you.

Anger
>Aren't you in control, God?
>Heal her or else!
>She believes you will
>Why aren't you doing it?
>This isn't fair or right
>You are wrong
>What's the point of praying?
>Heal her today!

Chemo, I resent you.

Guilt
>   I should do more
>   I can't help her
>   Desperation rules
>   Is this my fault?
>   God, please heal her
>   Hopelessness aches
>   Where's my faith?
Life, I despise you.

Depression
>   Hollow heart
>   Empty soul
>   Barren rooms
>   Why go on?
>   Barren home
>   Hollow faith
>   Take me too
Cancer, I hate you.

Grief is a path
>   A journey
>   With an exit
>   To a new normal
>   I don't want it
>   I want her
>   Not heartache
>   Loneliness
>   Life can't go on
>   I'm broken
>   Without her care
I'll never find

Acceptance

Part Three
August

Are We There Yet?

The leather-wrapped steering wheel of her Volvo SUV fit perfectly beneath her palms. Krista White tried to focus on the feel of it since it was pretty much the only perfect thing in her life at the moment. But the fingernail imprints from her tightening grip stole even that small joy.

Since she'd volunteered to drive, Krista didn't want to complain. The forty-minute drive from her house over the Lewis and Clark Bridge to Lacey's duplex in Castle Rock had been calm, and she'd listened to her favorite podcast for educators.

Now, not even an hour into the drive to Port Angeles, she couldn't recall why she'd agreed to this trip.

She reminded herself of her promise to Dad and Todd to reconcile with Lacey. Fulfilling her mother's final wish for a girls' trip to Vancouver Island was a second good reason for continuing when she wanted to turn around.

Already? The bitter voice of condemnation in her head

listed every fault and flaw.

I can't do this alone. I need help.

The furtive prayer pushed back the self-recriminations, but she'd consider it a miracle if they made it through the clog of traffic that marked the southern edge of Tacoma. Who could concentrate when every comment from her sister seemed to echo the litany from her inner critic?

Merci pointed out another crazy sign.

Lord bless that girl. She'd been trying so hard to pull them into the alphabet game or reminiscing about trips they'd taken to Mt. St. Helens when they'd driven past that exit. But Lacey's sullen silence dampened any attempt to lighten the atmosphere. Krista tried to chuckle at her niece's anecdotes from her job at the boutique.

"How goes the job search, Aunt K?" Merci's gum-chewing stretched the pause before she said Krista's name.

Krista gripped the wheel harder. Of course her niece would bring up the subject Krista wanted to avoid. Even talking about Mom's passing and the rift with her sister might be preferable to discussing this open wound. Maybe she'd be ready to admit her ultimate failure after a few days breathing Canadian air. Krista had nothing to show for all her sacrifices, which included her friendship with her sister. Her long-awaited dream to be a teacher mocked from some unattainable pinnacle, reinforcing the guilt she replayed from the day her mother had graduated to Heaven.

She gulped, sipping from her water bottle while collecting her thoughts. Not that any amount of time or thought would change her answer.

"A few interviews, but no job." Krista glanced in the rear-view mirror and met her niece's hazel gaze. She recognized the touch of desperation she saw there. Was her panic as apparent?

The trip wasn't going well for any of them, and they hadn't even left the country.

"Any feelers out?" Merci blew a bubble that popped before Krista replied.

"The local high school—my top choice —has asked me to do a long-term sub job for a teacher going on maternity leave." She sighed. Todd had told her it would get her foot in the door, but it felt like a nibble of bread to a starving person. "But I don't want to quit my job until I have a permanent position."

"Why does that matter?" Lacey's glare scorched Krista. "You don't have to work."

Krista bristled at the animosity. Even if she deserved it for not being there for Mom and Dad as much as she should have, it hurt. What had she done to cause Lacey to despise her so?

"Teaching is her dream job," Merci said.

Krista opened her mouth and shut it. What could she add to the conversation?

"Why shouldn't she have her dream?" Her niece leaned forward to give her mother the side-eye.

"I didn't say she shouldn't. I just don't see the big deal about quitting the credit union and going on the substitute list." Lacey sighed with dramatic effect and shrugged. "It's not like she needs the money."

Hearing them discuss her in third person made Krista grit her teeth. *I'm right here.*

But not ready to jump in. It was simpler to let the conversation flow around her. Her sister was entitled to an opinion. Maybe it was even accurate.

"Not everything is about money." Merci's tone went icy.

Krista glanced in the mirror, and their gazes connected again. This time her niece's was laced with apology. Krista gave a small shake of her head and focused on the string of brake lights ahead.

"We have two kids in college who might need financial help." Krista tried not to insert emotion into her statement, but her voice wavered a bit anyway.

She should have seconded Merci's sentiment. The Lord had blessed Todd with a lucrative job, and they'd always lived comfortably. But that hadn't kept the heartaches at bay. The important things in life couldn't be purchased.

Lacey huffed. "At least you're in a position to help. Try being so broke you can't even get your old car fixed." Lacey gave a false laugh, rubbing the soft leather seat. "Not that you drive an old car."

Krista cringed. She opened her mouth to offer to pay for her sister's car repairs. Closed it with a painful click of her back teeth. Every offer of financial assistance she or Todd had made since Lacey's divorce had been slapped down and treated as an affront to her independence.

And Krista didn't understand her sister's reluctance to borrow money from family. Everyone needed help sometimes. She and Todd had borrowed money from his parents to buy their first home. They'd paid it back, sure, but it wasn't held over their heads or brought up as an indictment against their adulting skills. Family helped family.

Krista took a deep breath, resolved to follow her inclination to help. "Todd and I are happy to lend you money, Lace. You know that." Her voice was low, apologetic.

"I don't need charity."

"A loan isn't charity, Mom." Merci leaned forward and laid her hand on Lacey's shoulder. "You've helped me and Lucas out lots of times. This isn't any different."

"I'm your mother. Parents are supposed to help their kids."

"Family helps family." Merci used a firm tone that reminded Krista of Mom. Maybe it was because the sentiment was a familiar one from her mother.

A pang of loss fanned the flames on Krista's simmering guilt. She should have spent more time with Mom, even if the hospital-like atmosphere had shriveled her insides.

"Leave it alone, Merci." Lacey shot a withering look over her shoulder, and Merci drew back as if her hand had been slapped.

Krista's stomach plunged under the seat. What had she done? This trip was a mistake. They couldn't even have a civil conversation on the drive to the resort. How would they survive a week together?

Contemporary Christian music surged into the ominous silence. Krista tried to focus on the lyrics.

Her thoughts whirled. They were going to be stuck together for the next week. And they were supposed to be taking this trip to honor Mom. She wouldn't have allowed this bickering.

I wish you were here, Mom.

Traffic opened up, and several miles flew past before Krista found the courage to speak.

"What sort of things do you want to see while we're there?"

After a long-suffering exhalation, Lacey said, "Butchart Gardens. Mom loved them." Her attention remained out the side window.

No surprise about that choice. Krista didn't love to garden, considering she had a black thumb, but she wanted to see the gardens, too. Her mother had extolled their glory quite often in the months since scheduling the trip.

Krista's throat tightened. She swallowed back the emotion which ambushed her at the oddest moments.

Merci pulled out her phone. Apparently, she searched online because after a minute, she tossed out ideas for places to see and things to do in Victoria. Her niece's enthusiasm sparked as she mentioned two castles that offered tours and several art museums.

"What day is the tea?" Merci glanced at Krista in the mirror.

"Friday afternoon." She'd entered the time on her calendar after Dad made the reservations a few weeks earlier.

"The second to last day." Merci hummed and tapped her chin. "Nothing like letting the anticipation build."

"Tea and crumpets please," Krista said in a false British accent.

Merci's laugh billowed, spilling joy through the tense atmosphere.

Krista's lips curled the slightest bit. Humor could redeem this vacation. She'd hoped and prayed her niece would be able to infuse lightheartedness into the trip.

Thank you, Lord.

Her shoulders relaxed, and she eased her death grip on the steering wheel. God had a plan for this vacation. It might not be what Mom had intended since she wasn't present to steer the ship, but it could be a time of healing. They all had grief to exorcise, and the chasm between the sisters needed a bridge.

"We should visit the gardens tomorrow," Lacey said. Her tone had thawed but she kept her gaze fixed on the passing scenery.

"Don't we want to have a down day before we go full steam ahead?" Krista never liked to hit the ground running on vacation. She preferred to use the first day to get her bearings and make a plan for the trip.

"I don't. I want to see the gardens." Lacey twisted toward the back seat. "How much does it cost to get in? Do we have to reserve a time?"

Merci and Lacey discussed details for the Butchart Gardens. Krista attempted to release the tension coiled like a striking snake in the pit of her stomach. She only had a single vote while traveling with other people. Still, it hurt that her wish had been brushed aside without due consideration.

Her breath caught.

Things would have been different if Mom was there. Oh yes, she would have itemized the itinerary and distributed copies of the battle plan. Her mother might have provided two or three choices and asked for input, but she would have made the final decisions.

In that scenario, Krista still would have been outvoted. She rubbed her breastbone, hoping to alleviate the ache in her heart. Since the trip was Mom's idea and she was the only one who'd traveled to Victoria before, Krista wouldn't have argued. She would have been fine going with the flow.

Nothing seemed fine now. Especially not taking the trip without her.

"Not far from the resort, there's a castle that has tours." Merci's tone sounded girlish. "Every princess needs to visit a castle, right?"

"Right," Krista agreed.

"How much does it cost?" Lacey's obsession with prices doused the warming enthusiasm.

"My treat," Krista said, and she wouldn't let her sister decline the offer.

Merci nodded. "There's a cool museum I want to see. I'll pay for us to visit that."

Which meant Lacey would want to purchase tickets to keep things equitable. Surely there was something relatively inexpensive her sister would enjoy seeing. Krista communicated her question with a raised eyebrow toward her niece, who answered with a shrug.

"I can stay at the condo," Lacey said, "while you do those things. I told you I can't afford this trip."

"Nonsense," Krista said. "It's vacation. Why can't you accept a gift?"

"It doesn't feel like a gift." Lacey's voice had lost its heat, but she clenched her hands in her lap.

Krista gripped the wheel, and her nails gouged her palms. With the pressure cooker of her irritation nearing the danger zone, she should agree to let Lacey pout in the condo.

"Mom!" Merci's squeal had Krista's shoulders driving to her ears. "They have a historic schoolhouse. We should see that."

Merci read the description. Lacey relaxed into her seat. Krista wanted to kiss her niece for finding a suitable distraction. Her stomach unclenched, although she suspected the subject of sharing expenses wasn't closed.

Krista hated that money had become a sore spot between them. Was it because Lacey had to struggle so much on her own?

Well, that was her choice. She hadn't even let Todd pay the deposit on her rental in Castle Rock. They couldn't force her to accept financial assistance. Either way, Krista couldn't see how Lacey's money issues were her fault, and it hurt to be treated as if they were.

Lacey had accepted some help from their parents, but it wasn't like anyone could keep Mom from doing what she set her mind to.

Krista's nose burned, and a veil of moisture clouded her vision. She blinked it away. The constant ache of missing Mom had faded to these unexpected slams of emotional agony. Who could predict what triggered the onslaught? Not Krista. If she could, she'd avoid them until she could grieve privately.

Hadn't she wept in public enough? When she teared up, people around her grew uncomfortable. Todd had assured her that was not her concern, but she disagreed. She didn't want to do something she knew made others uneasy. Especially not here and now when her weeping could trigger disgust and accusation from her sister.

"What do you think, Aunt K?"

Krista jerked herself from tearful reveries.

"I like to have down time to read by the pool." That was true enough and everyone in the car knew it. "How about if that's something you and your mom do together?" As if her mom wasn't sitting three feet away.

Krista cringed. As much as she resented being referred to in third person, she shouldn't do it to her sister. There would never be a bridge back to their close relationship unless one of them laid the first brick.

"Only two tickets to buy, Mom," Merci said.

"How will we get there if Krista isn't driving?"

Before Krista could offer the loan of her car, Merci volunteered information about a water taxi service. They could enjoy a great tour of the harbor before arriving at a dock near the school.

Should she change her mind? Krista could feel her mother frowning down on her decision. With a shake of her head, Krista brushed the sensation away. She had suggested the outing for Merci and Lacey with the upside being Krista could relax in relative silence.

If the tension in the car was an indicator, there might be more snappish exchanges or strained silences in the days ahead. Hopefully, Lacey would relax once they spent time in the center of Mom's plan. Otherwise, sharing a small condo for a week would be the opposite of a relaxing vacation.

Lord, I need more than perfect timing for the conversation I don't want to have with my sister. I need a survival plan.

With the exit for the ferry dock finally in sight, she sighed in relief. They'd get out and walk around the deck during that ninety-minute segment of the trip.

Are we there yet? Her sons had asked it often enough. She prayed silently that she would stop regretting her decision to take this trip.

Please, God. For Mom.

Because Krista needed a break already.

The Lady in the Garden

Sunshine smiled down on Lacey Bloom as she inhaled the fragrance of dozens of flowers. Somehow, she had survived spending time in close quarters with her sister the past two days, and today she reveled in her reward: solitary time in the Eden of Butchart Gardens.

Although they'd entered the garden together, Krista and Merci had agreed to go separate ways in the massive acreage located several miles outside of the city of Victoria. It made sense because everyone wanted to see different things. Lacey yearned to experience everything, but she didn't want to listen to her sister's inane commentary or her daughter's not-so-subtle attempts to lighten the mood. Lacey needed silence to soak in the sanctuary of this place her mother had loved.

Since arriving on Vancouver Island, Lacey had resorted to hiding in the condo's master bedroom or diving into a novel—although she wasn't certain what she'd read—to avoid interacting with her sister. Each morning, Lacey swam laps in the resort's short, shallow pool. Mealtime with her sister and daughter had meant biting her tongue and forcing smiles at their banter. She'd cooked their dinners to stay busy, and while the other two did the dishes, she'd walked along the waterfront.

Each night she'd stayed out longer to avoid playing games. Mom had taught them so many games, and Lacey usually loved playing them. The thought of enjoying them without Mom made the emptiness ache inside of Lacey. Even worse, the cavalier interaction between Merci and Krista made it seem like they didn't miss Mom or were trying too hard to fill the silence.

Lacey mentally shook off the oppressive thoughts and drank in the visual wonderland. The beauty of creation around her overshadowed the wreckage of her family life. The hollow in her soul from missing her mother cried out while words to the old hymn about walking and talking with God in the garden repeated through her mind.

Where were you, God? It was an accusation not a prayer, spurred from a lifetime of habit. Or so Lacey told herself.

When her mother's health had taken a downward turn, anger toward a supposedly present and loving God burned through the pain of abandonment. How could he snatch life from a godly woman who'd served him faithfully? That wasn't even considering the fact that his church people had ostracized Lacey without ever asking for her side of the story.

She pushed aside the hurtful thoughts. Today she would walk where Mom had walked and see this oasis of flowers through her eyes.

A sign at intersecting paths pointed toward the rose garden. Mom had loved roses. She'd curated a dozen rose bushes and lovingly tended them for years.

A pair of gray-haired ladies passed Lacey, heading away from the rose garden, chattering about the quantity of pink roses. She quickened her steps. Would there be multiple shades of yellow roses, too? Those were her favorite, while Mom had preferred peachier shades. When Lacey had moved into the house where she'd raised her children, Mom brought bare root rose bushes as a housewarming gift.

Each spring, Mom had helped Lacey dig around them for optimal fertilizing. When the leaves browned, Mom showed her how to treat spots and aphids. One bush produced sunny yellow blooms and the other pale peach flowers. In the fall, Mom returned with pruning shears to cull the branches and get the precious bushes ready for winter. The rich soil connected the roots of their hearts.

Was it any wonder Lacey's heart had died in January? The abrupt severing of their soul-deep bond had caused an agony she hadn't known existed. Worse even than the divorce and the subsequent death of her social circle.

But mooning over the past wasn't the point of this day. Today, she would wander among the rose bushes. She'd imagine Mom at her side, and they would soak in the beauty, discuss the variety, and share a few moments enjoying a garden. Together.

That's all she wanted. Another afternoon among the flowers they loved, to say what she hadn't been able to say because she hadn't been there for her mother's final breath. No, Krista had gotten that honor. And despised it.

The volcano of emotional conflict with her sister bubbled, feeling a bit like a bad case of heartburn. Sure, her sister had given lip service during the amputation of Lacey's marriage, but she'd been too absorbed in her own life to be a dependable resource. And when Mom went on hospice, Krista had continued forward with her student teaching like things were business as usual. Her sister had shattered only after Mom died, leaving Lacey to shoulder the fallout alone. Always alone.

Lacey shook herself, ignoring the churning cesspool of unspoken words and unresolved feelings. Today, she was in the most gorgeous garden in North America, yards away from more varieties of roses than she'd ever seen. She pushed aside the memories of past hurts and reminded herself to seek connection with her mother in a place they both loved.

The walkway curved beneath an archway of various pink roses climbing trellises. The scent Shakespeare wrote about swirled around her. She drank in the beauty, and something imperceptible loosened inside her. How she missed working in her garden.

She strolled beneath the canopy of roses. Beyond them, blue sky painted a perfect backdrop. Sunlight brightened the tender petals.

Awe and amazement misted over Lacey as she continued along the pathway. She snapped photo after photo, wondering how she would ever decide which bloom was her favorite. An incredible array of pink roses from palest carnation to hot pink lipstick surprised and delighted her.

"You would love this one," she said, snapping a shot of a vibrant medium-toned rose. "You were always a purist."

A gentle breeze carried a mix of flowery scents to her nose. Lacey stilled and closed her eyes. The wind's invisible fingers brushed the back of her hand. As if Mom's spirit touched her.

Instead of bringing tears to her eyes, the thought

released a lock on her soul. In this place, she could find peace.

I miss you, Mom. Please walk this path with me.

Her eyes flickered open and beheld a world of yellow rosebuds. They came in shades ranging from the barest hint of the gold to rich butter to hot August sunlight. A gasp parted her lips. With her phone, she snapped a panoramic photo, hoping to cement the moment of wonder in her heart. She never wanted to forget the joy surging through her chest at the beauty of her favorite color in bloom.

Carefully, she rounded the yellow section, hardly giving her camera app a rest. Each shade of yolk or marigold or sunflower delighted her, igniting a spark she'd been unwilling to acknowledge for months. Life bubbled inside.

"Oh, look at this one," she whispered, reaching toward a golden bloom. "This is the epitome of a summer day."

Wind tickled the leaves, like a head nod from her mom. Lacey leaned close to the bright blossom noticing a lemony tang underlying the floral aroma.

Yellow bled into red. Most people favored these flowers as signs of true love. The shades ranged from poppy to burgundy, breathtaking for sure, by not as stunning as the yellows had been. Lacey's phone didn't get raised as frequently, although she felt an urge to stop by a vine of blood red blossoms.

"You would like this," she muttered to her mother. "It's unique."

Near the stem, the bud looked fire engine red but the center appeared orange. Many florists offered roses with color only on the tips of their petals, but those were dipped in dye. She'd never realized roses in nature could grow with more than one shade.

Lacey snapped a picture. The variegated bloom reminded her of tulips she and Krista had admired at a tulip farm a few years before. Would Krista admire the similarity this bloom carried to some of her favorite tulips?

The desire to ask her sister the question burned in her, but they hadn't really talked in ages. She accepted partial blame for that because she avoided conflict. She certainly didn't want to think about her hurt and anger now.

Lacey paused on the edge of an enormous oval flower bed. Roses lined the wall and a variety of other flowers in blue and purple tones populated the center. She'd taken several photos before it occurred to her that resentment hadn't accompanied the thoughts of her sister.

Her mouth relaxed into a true smile. Her heart jumped and pumped as an alien sensation spread down her neck and through her middle. Lacey basked in it like a cat following sunlight across a floor before she realized what it was. Named it. Peace.

An ugly absence of peace had dominated her life since she'd walked out of her marriage. She'd made the right decision, one essential to protecting her well-being, but upheaval had followed. And the place where she'd savored and soaked in peace—church— had been snatched away, too.

A breeze tickled through her hair, tossing the chin-length strands around her face. This garden was holy ground, a place of worship. Today, it served her better than any church building.

She closed her eyes against welling tears, but the vision of beauty imprinted on the back of her eyelids didn't restrain the hot liquid from flowing down her cheeks. A warm wind licked it away. She imagined God putting those tears in a bottle like one of her sister's favorite psalms said.

Her sister cried easily. Krista had wept openly at Mom's funeral and again when they cleared out her closet. And each time, the tears compelled Lacey to harden her heart against Krista. Because her sister didn't deserve to grieve when she'd avoided spending time with Mom during her last months of life.

Lacey grasped at the anger, but it slipped away. It didn't belong in this sacred space. Maybe the negative emotions didn't belong in Lacey's heart either. Was it time to address them in conversation so she could release them for good?

Doubt niggled in the pit of her stomach.

Her eyes popped open, and she shuffled down the path toward an expanse pocked with roses in every hue. A swell of emotion threatened to strangle her. A deep breath relieved the rising panic at the thought of talking things out with her sister.

To one side of the path, a figure knelt among the flowers. The woman's long-sleeved shirt billowed slightly. A straw hat with a crisp peach ribbon shaded her head, but a few white curls peeped over the collar of the shirt.

Lacey's heart lurched. She blinked and would have rubbed her eyes if she hadn't been holding her phone. That was Mom's hat.

The woman stood and picked up a kneeling cushion with one hand and a bucket with the other. Lacey dared not breathe as the woman turned toward her.

"Mom?" The question was whispered with soundless hope.

The round face and crinkling brown eyes beneath the wide brim of the familiar hat didn't belong to her mother. Of course they didn't. Her mother was gone. While Mom's spiritual essence might stroll through the roses with Lacey, her physical presence no longer existed on Earth.

"Hello, dear. Aren't they lovely?" The woman had a strong Canadian accent. She gestured with filled hands to the bushes surrounding her.

"Amazing." Tears tickled her eyes again, but Lacey widened them, trusting the tint of her glasses to keep any redness hidden. This stranger didn't deserve to endure the curse of her grief. Even more, this hallowed ground didn't need to be watered by weeping.

"There are technically only seven types of roses here. The colors and shapes make it seem like more."

The woman wove her way through the bushes, lighting on the path a few steps away from Lacey. Her navy slacks and black garden clogs bore signs of hours crawling through the detritus of browned leaves and weeds.

"Let me show you my favorite."

Lacey gulped and managed to whisper, "Okay."

"I don't mean to intrude." The woman's gloved hand shot toward her mouth, stopping short of actual contact. "Goodness. I need to get these off."

Lacey smiled at the hot pink gardening gloves protecting the woman's hands from cruel thorns. Her mismatched accessories appealed to Lacey, reminding her of the abundance of beauty surrounding them rather than the absence of her mother.

"You're not intruding. I'd love to see your favorite rose."

The woman settled her bucket and kneeler on the ground by her feet, freeing her hands to peel off the gloves. She rolled them into a tidy package and tucked them away in a pocket of her voluminous red shirt.

"In that case, I'm Nan Ketch." She extended her

wrinkled, spotted hand with short nails and calloused palms.

"Lacey Bloom."

"Bloom? Like a flower's bloom?"

Lacey's mouth quirked upward. "Exactly like that."

"What a fabulous name!"

The woman's enthusiasm gave Lacey pause. She'd been thinking of reclaiming her maiden name. Today, though, the name felt like a perfect fit.

When they shook, Nan's hand was cool.

"Pleased to make your acquaintance." She carried her gardening paraphernalia to a bench Lacey hadn't noticed, tucking it under the seat. "On to the coral."

They walked side-by-side beneath another path covered in red, white, and yellow roses. The colors screamed cheer. Lacey hoped the feeling would soak deeply inside and remain once she left this magical place.

The pathway split. Rose-covered arches continued forward, but Nan turned down the left-hand walk. They stopped in front of a tall, nearly tree-like plant adorned with buds hanging at eye level. The flowers weren't peach, salmon, or orange but a perfect coral color.

"Coral Wind. Who would choose pink when you could have coral." The woman gestured to shorter, bushier plants filling the bed with riots of pinks and reds.

"I can see why you love this color." Lacey leaned close and inhaled, but instead of the typical rosy scent, she smelled a bouquet of fruit.

"What do you smell, Miss Bloom?"

Lacey cocked her head and pivoted her attention to Nan. "Fruit. But nothing I can pinpoint."

The woman nodded and pursed her lips. "I think it's the Creator's way of distinguishing among the colors. Even a blind person could appreciate the differences."

True beauty for all the senses. That's what she'd found in this garden. Even more, proof that she'd been wrong to discount God's existence because her life hadn't gone according to plan. These moments could be nothing but a gift that from God.

Thank you.

For once, she didn't rebel at the thought of prayer. Was it possible to struggle with faith while still appreciating the magnificence crafted by God?

"Reds and pinks smell more like the traditional rosy scent people expect." The woman bobbed her head, and the peach ribbon fluttered, drawing Lacey's attention back to the familiar hat.

She'd given her mother that gardening hat's twin after she'd started cancer treatment. Every chemotherapy drug she'd taken carried a warning to limit or avoid exposure to sunlight but being banished from the garden would have been worse than a death sentence for Mom. So, they'd gone on a mission to find clothing and gloves with built-in sun protection, UV rated at 70 SPF or higher.

Lacey missed the list of fragrance possibilities Nan relayed, but she snapped photos and shuffled along beside her exuberant guide.

A neon orange bud blinded her.

"Whoa!" She lifted her phone and took a picture.

"Marquee," Nan said. "Like on Broadway in New York City."

"It's perfect." Lacey leaned close to get a shot of the intricate curl of the petals.

A bee buzzed up from the center. Lacey stumbled backward, fumbling with her phone as she waved her arms to ward off an attack.

"They love the brightest ones," Nan said, her tone soft, nearly drowned by Lacey's suddenly pounding heart.

"I should have remembered that."

"Are you allergic?" Nan's brow creased with worry.

"No. My daughter is, so I'm glad she's somewhere else and not as likely to stick her nose in a flower."

Nan chuckled. The sound tingled along Lacey's arms, melting the iceberg around her heart. She flashed the woman an authentic smile, and more internal armor crumbled to dust.

"Now, I should show you Bonnie Blue. She's the rose everyone comes to see."

Although Lacey wanted to protest since she hadn't explored this section as much as she would have liked, Nan pulled her along in a tide of excitement.

A thin plant with four scrawny branches, a bud on the end of each, sat isolated in a raised bed. Miniature roses covered the ground around it, their vines stretching in all directions, blooms in pink, white, and red rioting to cover the soil.

A single blue bud drooped from the very top of the sick-looking bush. Cobalt blue petals, looking as soft and rich as a velvet jeweler's box, startled the eye. Beauty among the ashes.

Like your life.

Emotion punched her breastbone, and Lacey gasped. She'd never seen a flower so incredible. Words fled. None seemed worthy of expressing the awe evoked by the gem on that stem.

Several beats of silence passed. Voices from the path beyond the roses hummed in static. Finally, the rasp of her breathing jerked Lacey out of the stupor.

"Unspeakable beauty," Nan said, her voice hushed, as if they'd entered an ancient cathedral.

Lacey wanted to stroke the gorgeous bloom, certain it would be velvety, but she gripped the side of her khaki walking shorts instead. The designers had placed it out of reach, as if aware its beauty would hypnotize and draw unwelcome hands.

Unspeakable beauty. But its scraggly foliage told a different story.

"What's wrong with it?" No other plant she'd seen looked as small and unhealthy. Shouldn't it be the opposite? This was the crown jewel of the rose garden, so it should be thriving.

"Nothing." Nan chuckled as surprise jolted through Lacey. "The plant is fragile. You can see the branches have no thorns."

Lacey squinted, raising her sunglasses and leaning closer. The branches didn't appear woody, and where thorns usually lined the stalks, a fuzzy looking stubble dotted the stems instead. Bonnie Blue looked like a strong breeze could blow her off her private knoll.

"Why?" A strange urge to shelter the plant pushed against Lacey's soul.

"In finding the right DNA to make this startling blue shade, the botanists ended up stripping the plant of its woody stalk and thorny protection." Nan frowned. "Poor Bonnie can't seem to grow more than four branches."

"Will she get stronger?"

Nan shrugged. "This is her second summer out in the garden. One among 280 varieties of roses. A special gardener checks the quality of the soil daily."

"Is that you?"

Nan laughed. The hearty sound shattered the blanket of amazement that had shrouded Lacey at the incredible sight of the blue rose.

"Not hardly." A rueful smile pinched Nan's thin lips. "I'm a volunteer. I can't get enough of these blooms, so I weed once or twice per week in the growing season."

"I love working in flower beds, too. It's something my mom and I did together." Lacey wanted to call the words back, afraid they'd invite Nan to ask questions she didn't want to answer. But the attempt was futile since what is said can never be unspoken.

A litany of harsh barbs she'd aimed at Krista rang in her mind. She cringed as the echo dimmed the light of peace found in the garden.

"Then you understand." Nan's rough hand patted Lacey's forearm, and her eyes darkened in kinship.

Lacey hardened herself, preparing for a stream of meaningless platitudes.

Nan's hand fell away. "This flower, though beautiful, has a precarious place in the world. Like each of us."

A precarious place. Life came with zero guarantees for longevity. Mom had lived seventy fulfilling years because she knew how to embrace living. Lacey had stopped living months before the fateful text came from her sister.

Lacey's choices weren't Krista's fault. Yes, the fact that Krista had chosen school over time with Lacey had hurt, but Lacey still needed her. Now that Mom was gone, Lacey needed Krista more than ever. So why did she keep pushing her away?

"Thank you for showing me your favorite rose. And Bonnie Blue."

Nan bobbed her head. "Always enjoy meeting someone who appreciates this place."

Nan waved, heading back to her abandoned items. Lacey photographed the show-stopping blue rose, zooming in to capture its velvety quality. She leaned closer, trying to sniff out its peculiar aroma, but with all the roses around, there was no way to catch the scent.

She thumbed through the pictures on her screen, amazed again by the fragile plant that produced such a spectacular flower.

Fragile like life. Like her tender heart.

I am strength. A breeze whispered around her, as if carrying the gentle voice from heaven.

She plopped on a nearby bench and searched for her Canadian guide, but the woman was gone. Maybe Nan had been an angel. Her message echoed in the ghost town of Lacey's soul.

"I miss you, Mom." She realized that Bonnie Blue would not have been here when her parents visited a few years ago. "Did you see that blue rose?"

A butterfly winged past, alighting on a white rose. Life swelled around her.

Was it time to wake up? She'd been going through the motions—work, school, sleep.

Emotion clogged her throat. She permitted a tear to fall. It hit the back of her hand and rolled off onto the grass. Out of sight. Like the vapor of human life.

Mom might be gone but Lacey believed she still lived. Maybe she was cultivating a rose garden in Heaven.

Another breeze stirred, stroked her skin, and dried her tears.

Thanks for being here, Mom.

Why are you angry with your sister? The question echoed in Mom's voice. Perhaps because Lacey had heard her ask it only days before she'd passed from this life to the next. Lacey had avoided the topic then because it didn't seem important in light of Mom's limited hours of life.

But hearing it here, Lacey realized it had been the most important thing her mother had wanted to know. She breathed in summer's sweetness and allowed the question to penetrate through the protective layers over her heart.

This time, as Lacey considered her relationship with Krista, the usual anger and hurt didn't engulf her. The garden had replaced those negative emotions with peace and hope. Would that good remain when she stepped off this sacred ground?

Please. Let it be real.

Her heart leaped at the prayer.

More than fledgling faith and rose-scented air, she needed to build a bridge back to her sister. In this garden, for the first time, she believed such a feat of relational engineering possible.

More than a Field Trip

Failure loomed over Mercedes Bloom like a dark cloud against the sunny Canadian sky. Time ticked on, and her promise to Grandma weighed on her heart and mind. Since Mom and Aunt K could barely speak to each other, Merci needed to step into the gap.

Jesus, I need Grandma's wisdom.

Genius didn't fall from Heaven in answer to her plea. What she really wanted was Grandma. If she were here, Merci knew they wouldn't be four days into this trip with the sisters reading in separate spaces every night. Instead, there would be nightly games that included all of them, heart-to-heart conversation, and laughter.

She missed the laughter most of all.

Aunt K had the day reading by the pool she wanted, and Merci knew she needed to be proactive.

Lord, let this time open a door.

Merci had suggested visiting the oldest schoolhouse on Vancouver Island with her mother more to reconnect to their past than learn Canada's history. The "field trip" akin to some they'd taken during her home school days provided conversation starters. Without her aunt along, Merci hoped those private conversations would provide a way to talk about the unmentionable subject— the rift between her mom and aunt.

With a sigh, Merci wiped sweat from her brow and followed her mother to the stairway inside the old schoolhouse. Craigflower Historic Site had been a homestead and school since the 1800s. In its nod to remaining authentic, it didn't have air conditioning, so the upper level's stifling heat glued her cotton shirt to her back.

With the exit in sight, Merci fought the urge to make a break for the outdoors. Surely it would be cooler outside.

Mom held the wooden door leading to the back stoop. "How about visiting the cheese-making booth first?"

A breeze carried the odor of goats and wood chips from a line of tents beyond the woodshed in the back yard. The first pungent scent took her back to working with her childhood best friend at the fair. The other put her in the middle of Grandpa's workshop while he cut forms for a wooden Nativity set Grandma would paint.

I wish you were here, Grandma. You'd know how to get this conversation started.

Mom led the way. "It's interesting that this farm hosted agricultural experiments for the Hudson Bay company. You remember learning about their outpost in Astoria?"

Merci nodded. "That was a fun field trip. Until Lucas whined about climbing up the Astoria Column."

"He was only six."

Merci grimaced. "He always was your favorite."

Mom swatted at her. "My favorite son for sure." It was an old joke between them, and since Mom played along,

Merci hoped her intervention plan would work.

She credited that near smile on Mom's face to whatever had happened at Butchart Gardens the day before. Aunt K had suggested they split up when it became clear that each of them had different priorities about what to see. Merci had wandered through the gardens, sitting on benches and soaking in the delicious sights and sounds.

At the end of their visit, Mom had rejoined them a few minutes late. Not that they cared since she had been relaxed and talkative, mostly going on about the roses she'd seen. Merci had hoped her mother's change would lead to a conversation between the sisters at the condo that night, but while Aunt K talked on the phone with Uncle Todd, Mom had retired to her room to read. Again.

Merci had sent frustrated messages to Stephan, who encouraged her to let that day go and consider how she could facilitate their conversation later. That had given Merci the idea of broaching the subject head-on during her time alone with her mom.

Mom's shoulders were relaxed, and she hadn't snapped about anything all day. Merci crossed her fingers, taking this as a sign Mom was primed for the all-important reckoning with Aunt K.

Merci's feet screamed for rest. She might stand eight hours per day at her retail job, but she'd clocked more miles in the past two days than she walked in two weeks at the mall. Sadness dimmed the bright day for a moment. Things were about to change for her, and she'd miss the mall vibe. Mostly, she'd miss her employee discount at Your Plus One.

After listening to the spiel from the cheese makers, Merci announced, "I need a drink."

Mom stopped midway to the wood crafting display. Her

face sagged with disappointment, but she turned back with a slight nod. "We can check out the other booths later."

Merci expected the memories in the woodworker's booth might overwhelm her, and she needed all her wits to carry out her plan. Although getting the most out of their admission price would be her mother's goal, Merci cared less about seeing all the things, especially if it hindered what needed to happen.

Mom followed her to the refreshment stand, an actual food truck parked away from the period displays. A roped-off area of chairs and tables offered a place to sit and enjoy the food and drink.

While Mom snagged a table, Merci stood in the short line. How would she approach the subject of reconciliation? Could anything they saw today help her turn the conversation toward Aunt K?

After purchasing a lemonade for each of them, Merci prayed her way to the round Bistro table where her mother waited. She set the drinks down, pulled out a wooden folding chair, and dropped heavily into the seat. A sigh spilled from her lips, echoing the relief in her feet.

She studied her mother as they both tore the covers off their straws. Merci sipped the tart drink, lips puckering at the tang. How could she drive the conversation where she needed it to go? Should she ask outright?

Lord, I really need help.

Mom drank some juice and smacked her lips. "This museum brought back some great memories of our homeschool days, didn't it? To think some people thought I was holding you back, but you're a college graduate."

This wasn't the direction Merci wanted the conversation to go.

"I was as prepared for college as any of the traditionally educated people," she said. This wasn't a new subject for them, but maybe reinforcing Mom's parenting choices would open a door.

Before Merci could continue with a compliment, Mom stared her in the eye and said, "Tell me about school. You haven't said much about your most recent class. When does fall term start?"

Merci stared at her paper cup. She had no desire to talk about school. But if coughing up this secret became the gateway for the more important topic, it would be worth it. She shrugged. "Don't know. I'm not going."

Mom's eyebrow raised, and she leaned closer. "Excuse me? I thought I heard you say you're not going."

Merci nodded because her voice had deserted her. She so didn't want to hear the next words out of her mother's mouth.

"Mercedes Louise Bloom!"

Merci's lips quirked upward. The full name treatment would likely be the best part of this lecture.

"Why aren't you going to school? Is this about money?" Mom drummed her fingers. "I don't understand why your father is such a tightwad. Just because he doesn't have—"

Merci held up her hand. "Dad has nothing to do with it. He doesn't even know." And she certainly didn't want to have any sort of conversation about her father with her mother.

In the year since the divorce, Merci had avoided any conversations about the other parent or the divorce. It didn't feel proper to say she understood why Mom left, or that both of them seemed happier apart.

If Grandma hadn't made Merci promise, she wouldn't

be getting in the middle of her mom's problems with Aunt K either. Merci liked relationships to be fun and easy. When two people accepted each other no matter what, things flowed. It had been that way with Grandma. And it was that way with Stephan, too.

"Then...I don't understand. You have a psychology degree for the sole purpose of being a Christian counselor. But that requires a graduate degree."

Merci huffed, holding back an eye roll because she knew it would irritate her mother. "Not telling me anything I don't already know." And she didn't appreciate the reminder that the $80,000 undergraduate degree was useless on its own.

Her stomach knotted. How would she pay back her student loans? Without a job, it didn't look possible. That was one of the benefits of continuing her education she'd miss. In a few months, she'd have to figure it out.

"What is this about?" Mom straightened. "If not money, then what?"

"I'm not a good fit for counseling."

Mom had the look of a stray cat about to bolt.

"Seriously. When I worked at the suicide hot line..." Her throat closed. She didn't want to go there.

"Oh, honey. A suicide hot line is not a good barometer." Mom patted Merci's hand and then squeezed it. "Don't decide your future based on that."

Merci shook her head and swiped her eyes with her free hand. "The internship at the Eastside Christian Middle Grade Academy didn't go well either."

"Middle school! Kids that age wouldn't pretend to be grateful even if you solved all their problems."

She wasn't wrong. But Merci recalled freezing up the day a girl talked to her about physical abuse from her "uncle."

She couldn't deal with stories or situations like that. Once the girl had left the office, Merci hyperventilated. After tearfully explaining things to the mentor counselor, she'd taken the rest of the day off.

"I don't want to hear about the horrors of another person's life. Especially not a kid."

Silence swirled between them. Merci smiled at an older couple who sat at a nearby table. Wind picked up, blowing her hair back and drying her scalp. She was glad of the fluttering cover over this section of tables which shaded her from the sun's burning rays as well as its heat.

"I'm sure you could specialize in something that would help you avoid all that." Her mother gave a disgusted grunt. "You're smart and have a degree. I hate to see you wasting yourself at that retail job."

Well, wouldn't she be surprised to learn that wasn't happening either? *What about being unemployed, Mom? How does that sit with you?*

"Look at me, Merci. I'm a textbook example of why girls need to get degrees and pursue careers."

Irritation swamped Merci, drowning the fear of her other secret's revelation. "You were happy to be our mom and teacher. There's nothing wrong with that."

"Except I can't support myself now. I want more for you. You deserve more."

More what? Merci prayed she'd find what was missing once she spent more time with Stephan. He was a godly man who valued her abilities and encouraged her to follow her heart. Furthermore, he was nothing like her controlling father.

"Have you considered that? Do you have a plan? You need one." Mom's sympathy morphed into condemnation from one sentence to the next.

"I have a plan, Mom." But she wasn't ready to share it since it wasn't specific and wouldn't satisfy her mother. In fact, Mom probably wouldn't like it at all if that crack about needing a career was any indicator.

"You could be a teacher. You've always been great with little kids." Mom pushed her empty cup away. "I don't think your undergraduate degree matters that much if you get a MAT."

And there it was—her perfect opening.

Thank you, Jesus!

"I could ask Aunt K about that."

Mom froze. She nodded slowly and stared toward the exhibits, fumbling to pull a water bottle from her sling pack.

Merci straightened, pulled in a deep breath, and tossed a plea for help skyward. "Mom, what's up with you and Aunt K? You guys are best friends. Why won't you talk to her?"

Mom sat stiff and unblinking, gazing past Merci toward the historic buildings. Merci gulped another mouthful of lemonade, hoping it would infuse her with grit and gusto.

"She texted me to say your grandmother died." Mom's words rushed like air from a balloon and with similar force.

"Oh my." Merci frowned.

What a horrible way to learn of Grandma's passing. But Merci knew that wasn't the root of the trouble. Their problems had begun months earlier, and that's why Grandma had planned this trip. What wasn't Mom saying?

"She wasn't there for your grandmother. Claimed she hated hospitals and had too much schoolwork." The bitter tone deepened with every word.

Merci's heart plunged. "I didn't visit Grandma at the hospital the last few times she was in either, Mom. It's not everyone's—"

"You were in school."

"So was Aunt K. And she works full-time. Cut her some slack, Mom."

"Why? She encouraged me to leave your father and then—" Mom shut down, almost like someone had flipped an off switch.

A flock of hummingbirds pounded Merci's breastbone, trying to break free. She gulped. This thing with her mom and aunt had to do with the divorce? She tilted her head.

That didn't make sense. Her mom had stayed with Uncle Todd and Aunt K for a month or more. Had something happened between them while she stayed there?

Merci covered her mother's hands with hers and stared into her thin face, silently urging her mother to meet her gaze.

After what felt like a decade of silence, Mom looked at her. "I don't want to discuss the divorce with you. It's not right. You love your dad, and I won't put you in the middle." She shook her head. "It's bad enough that Lucas is living there and is always in the middle."

"I don't blame you for leaving Dad." Merci knew he was controlling and hard to live with. But he was the only father she had on earth. Good thing her Heavenly Father did a much better job of living up to the title.

"Thank you. It would have been nice if a few people at church had felt the same."

Merci stiffened and gritted her teeth. Oh, yes. She had plenty to say to the people at the church where her mother had worked so hard for years. That they would believe Mom had an affair—believe anything Dad said when he hardly darkened the church doors and disparaged the pastor every time he did. Well, not to his face. That wasn't how Dad worked.

"I'm sorry about that, Mom. Really. They give Christians everywhere a bad name."

Merci nearly gaped at the tears in her mother's eyes. Her mom didn't cry often. She'd only shed a few tears in Merci's sight since Grandma died, and never over anything Dad had said or done to her.

"Did Aunt K say something about that? The affair?"

Mom flinched. "What? No. She knows I didn't have an affair."

"Mom, what did she do? This thing between you started before Grandma got sick that last time."

Emotion welled up in Merci's throat. She wanted to ask more, press her mother for answers. It's what Grandma expected. What she'd promised to deliver.

God, I need Grandma. I can't do this.

Mom shifted and patted Merci's hands. "I'm getting hungry. What do they have to eat here?"

She stood and Merci trailed her to the food cart. Merci's legs weighed a ton, which seemed light compared to her heart. She'd failed Grandma again. She wasn't any closer to understanding the trouble between Mom and Aunt K or figuring out how to mend it.

Good thing she'd dropped out of school. If she couldn't intervene in this issue with her family, she had no business trying to help other people with their problems.

I'm sorry, Grandma.

Tick tock. Time for mending the broken relationship was running out.

Elephant in the Tearoom

Turquoise flashed in the mirror as Krista White exited her car. A shockwave buzzed into her empty stomach. The unfamiliar weight of her colorful beret—a gift from Mom—pressed against her head.

High tea at The Empress Hotel. A wistfulness choked against Krista's bubbling well of excitement.

I wish you were here, Mom.

She glanced to either side, but no one joined her.

At the hotel's entrance, Merci called over her shoulder, "Come on, Aunt K."

Her niece snatched her mother's arm, the sight reminding Krista of the distance between her and Lacey. Had she done all she could to reconcile with her sister? She replayed the previous evening.

Lacey marched past the kitchen where Krista leaned against the counter waiting for Merci to pass her a clean dish.

Her niece glanced her way, eyes wide. This was the moment they'd plotted for because if Lacey kept running away, the purpose of the trip would never be met.

"How about I join you on your walk?" Krista dropped the towel on the counter and moved in the direction of her sister.

Rather than answering, Lacey jerked open the door and rushed from the condo as if a grizzly bear was chasing her.

Krista blinked. Merci whirled toward her, dripping suds on the floor between them.

Another failure.

Krista's sandals clattered against the sidewalk, drawing her back to the present. The full skirt of her sundress whipped around her calves. A gust of wind stirred the scent of gas fumes mixed with saltwater.

A doorman nodded to her as she swept through the door he held. The brick facade with multiple towers screamed historic grandeur while the high ceilings and dark paneling of the lobby echoed with refinement.

She stared at gilded gauze creating the image of a bow around lights high above. A beam of sunlight spotlighted a hallway beyond the registration desk.

Another uniformed employee asked, "Afternoon tea?" before directing them into the Lobby Lounge.

Inside what Krista imagined a king's study to be like, a hostess led them through a maze of tables. She pulled out a chair with a crown-shaped back. A crushed velvet settee sat across from it, with a white cloth-draped table separating them.

Merci and Lacey slid onto the fancy love seat while Krista ducked her chin to the hostess before arranging her skirts over the padded chair and slipping her mini bag onto the empty seat beside her.

A pang twisted in her chest as her fingers lingered on the red cushion. Mom would be wearing her favorite peach hat with its silk flowers and a ribbon that nearly hung over the wide brim. The one her sister wore had a similar look but with a sage green ribbon and white silk flowers.

Krista glanced toward Merci's white hat and caught her niece staring at the empty seat. With trembling fingers, Krista opened a leather menu lying on the table in front of her.

She'd never seen anything like it. One side had see-through packets of tea leaves. Each was numbered and the corresponding numbers on the other half of the menu named and described the tea.

Krista gaped. She knew nothing about tea, but surely one didn't select it based on what the leaves looked like.

Lacey's eyes sparkled as she held the menu up and sniffed the packets of leaves.

"Hey, I've heard of Orange Pekoe." Merci frowned over the menu at her mother. "Can you actually smell them?"

A waiter dressed in black slacks and a white shirt appeared beside their table. "Is this your first tea at The Empress?"

Was it the fact her sister's nose was buried in the menu that gave them away?

He explained that tea would be brought out first. Krista glanced over the menu as he described the timing, allowing sufficient space between courses for the tea to steep. He pointed out the hourglass timers provided to ensure each brew reached the desired strength. Scones and jam arrived promptly after that, followed by the sandwich course, and finally the dessert tray.

A menu card described each dish.

"There will be three of each dessert?" Merci's eyes widened when their server responded affirmatively. "Is this

Heaven?"

For a split second, a grin broke through his serious demeanor.

"Any other questions about the menu? Any dietary restrictions I should be aware of?" When they shook their heads, he continued, "I'll be back shortly to take your tea order."

With a tip of his head, he turned away. He strode to a nearby table where three generations, from elementary-aged granddaughter in pigtails to silver-haired grandmother, had recently been seated.

A twinge in her chest tried to intrude, but Krista took a deep breath and frowned at the tea leaves. "I think I'll try the Imperial Breakfast tea."

Merci smirked as she handed over the hourglass with orange sand. "You can always turn it twice and see if the tea gets as strong as coffee."

Lacey's lips twisted. "I'd like that doves silver needle tea, but I can't believe it's ten dollars extra." She sighed. "It smells like peaches."

Not the money thing again. Krista didn't want to argue but this visit wouldn't come again. She gulped, praying for fortitude, and said, "How about if Todd covers upgrades?" Even if they all ordered more expensive tea, it wouldn't be more than fifty dollars.

Lacey blinked and opened her mouth, refusal clear in her expression. Merci's elbow nudged her mother's side. Lacey closed her mouth.

Interesting. Krista wondered what the two had discussed on their outing to that old school. Or maybe it was the atmosphere in the tearoom that stifled Lacey's negative comments.

In any case, Krista smiled at Merci, glad to have settled this small thing without an argument. It's what Mom would want.

Krista glanced at the empty chair beside her, wishing it wasn't vacant.

The server returned. Merci ordered Flora's Berry Garden for herself and interrupted her mother to order the silver needle.

"I have a note that this table has prepaid, but the additional charges aren't covered." The server glanced at each of them.

"I'll cover the upgraded tea," Krista said, ducking her chin in confirmation. "And stick with the imperial breakfast tea."

He gave an answering nod. "Lovely choices, ladies. The tea will be out momentarily." He gathered up the tea menus and departed.

Merci tapped her nail on the creamer carafe, which probably contained real cream rather than milk like many people used in the states.

Krista wondered what sort of tea Mom would have ordered, opened her mouth to ask, but a lump trapped her voice in the back of her throat. She sipped water, trying to clear it.

Before Krista could say anything, a girl wheeled a cart into the room, stopping at various tables to deposit teapots. Servers followed, answering questions.

At their table, she set three tea pots beside their matching cups. She named the teas and set a tea leaf strainer in each pot, settling the lids firmly in place. After she finished, the girl reached for the extra place setting to Krista's right. Krista covered the porcelain teacup with her hand, rocking it against its saucer.

The server's brown eyes widened as she met Krista's gaze. Krista shook her head, and the girl nodded and withdrew, leaving the dishes behind.

Your place is waiting, Mom.

Krista flipped her timer, noticing her sister used the white sanded one—meant for a medium brew. A teasing comment about tea drinkers rose in her mind but she squelched it. Their current relationship wasn't one that welcomed banter.

But I want to change that. Mom wanted me to.

The server stopped by the table, applauding them for finding the timers. He pointed out the four different sweeteners. Lacey asked something about the pink one.

"About the scones," Krista said when he shuffled backward. "I don't eat raisins."

"There are plain butter scones, as well," he assured her.

Lacey shook her head, waiting until he turned to the generational table before saying, "No raisins. Really?"

Krista's gaze clashed with her sister's. Although Lacey's tone said she was appalled that Krista had mentioned her life-long aversion in the fancy tearoom, it didn't carry the heat such comments had even one day before.

She didn't let her face show the hope jigging in her chest. "They're disgusting."

"Nothing in this place is disgusting." Lacey's tone was emphatic without carrying a bite of disapproval.

"Okay. They disgust me." It wasn't fair to call anything in the palace-like Lobby Lounge disgusting.

"I might pick them out." Merci smirked.

The twinkle in her eyes screamed joy. Approval surged around Krista, as if from an outside source. The fine hair on her arms jumped to attention.

She snuck a glance at the vacant seat, surprised to see it empty when she sensed a tangible presence beside her.

"Finally!"

Krista's heart hammered at her niece's exclamation. Merci poured tea into her cup. Lacey deliberately removed the strainer and placed it on the saucer before pouring her tea and stirring in a small portion of non-sugar sweetener.

Lacey lifted her cup to her chin and blew on the steam before sipping at the liquid. Her eyes closed, and her sharp features relaxed as she inhaled the mist.

"Too hot." Merci stirred her tea vigorously although she hadn't added any sweetener or cream. "How is it, Mom?"

Lacey kept the cup within range of her nose. "Smells delicious. Tastes fruity. A great choice."

"I hope mine tastes like berries." The spoon tinkled on the china cup as Merci continued to stir. "Why does it have to be so hot?"

"Hot drinks are best hot," Krista teased, tempted to ice down her tea since that's how she preferred it. But that wasn't part of the high tea experience.

"The flavor is different based on temperature," Lacey said. "I can taste all the different notes when it's hot."

Krista blinked. Is that why she didn't like hot tea? She'd never considered a reason for preferring iced tea.

A tug in her chest reminded her how much she missed her sister. They looked at things differently, and Krista loved hearing Lacey's observations.

Another server arrived with a plate holding six scones, four had raisins and the other two didn't.

"Perfect timing," Merci crowed.

Diners from nearby tables glanced in their direction.

Krista nodded at them, not embarrassed by the enthusiastic display. She could almost hear Mom asking Merci to use her inside voice.

Krista's lips quirked.

Merci put a scone on her plate and pulled the clotted cream and preserves close for easy access.

"What is clotted cream?" the girl wondered aloud, even as she spooned some onto the pastry.

"British butter," Krista said. "Well, actually, it's halfway between butter and whipped cream, so sweeter and creamier than butter."

"Too much will clog your arteries," Lacey said, spooning a generous portion on one half of the scone she'd sliced open.

Their gazes collided.

"What?" Lacey's hand froze.

Krista shook her head. Before their falling out, she might have made a joke about being glad for her dress' loose waistline, but she didn't know how this Lacey would receive it. And the realization tempered her joy.

She glanced down at her plate, breaking the awkward moment. "Who came up with a name like clotted cream?" She dropped a dollop on the plain scone on her plate.

Merci licked her lips. "Siri could tell us." She reached for her phone lying face down on the table beside her silverware.

Krista waved her off. "Rhetorical. Clotted anything sounds horrible. Not something I want to eat for sure." The pastry crumbled against her teeth and melted onto her tongue with the creamy topping. She smacked her lips. "I changed my mind. Better than butter."

"As if the scones were made for it," Merci agreed.

"More likely, the cream was fashioned for the scones." Lacey dabbed at the corner of her mouth with a napkin before sipping her tea. Her entire body sighed in contentment.

Krista smiled and glanced toward Mom's seat. A faint glow surrounded the chair. A trick of the lighting? Krista blinked to test that theory. Her breath caught as a vision of her mother raising an eyebrow hovered above the fancy chair. Another blink and it became a vacant chair once more.

"I might have died and entered bakery heaven," Merci said, clasping her free hand over her heart and closing her eyes in a false swoon.

Krista shook her head at her niece's dramatics. The comforting sense of Mom's presence remained beside her.

"More for me," Lacey said, biting into the raisin-speckled scone with abandon.

"That hurts." Merci cast sad eyes toward her mother before taking another bite.

Krista spooned strawberry preserves onto half her scone. After enjoying several bites, she announced, "Mom made better strawberry jam."

The memory of standing in the yellow kitchen of their old farmhouse reared into her mind with dizzying speed.

Krista stood on the wooden stump that served as a step stool to stir the bubbling pot of smashed strawberries while Mom slowly poured in the sugar.

"Keep stirring. You don't want it to scorch," she said.

"My arm is getting tired."

"This is hard work, but you can do it."

Lacey stood at the kitchen table, pausing with a masher suspended over a bowl of berries. Juice and pulp dripped from the metal tines. The sweet scent of berries and sugar filled the room.

Krista blinked and was back in the fancy tearoom. Mom had taught them so much.

Thanks, Mom. Are you here with us?

Krista cleared her throat. "I liked your blackberry syrup the best."

The sisters shared a meaningful look.

Krista prayed Lacey saw her sincerity. Hoped the tastes and smells of this moment brought those days spent harvesting berries and making jams and syrups to her sister's mind. They had been more than sisters, more than best friends.

Krista's stomach lurched. She wanted that back.

Lacey nodded slowly before pouring herself another cup of tea.

"I'm not usually a fan of scones," Merci said and slurped tea. "But these are tender and flaky."

Servers rolled carts into the room. One person set silver racks in the middle of the table. Their waiter arrived with a large plate displaying various finger sandwiches. He pointed out each one— salmon striploin on seven grain bread, chicken salad on a mini brioche, ham and cheese tartlet, and cucumber on dark rye—before sliding the platter onto the lowest tier of the serving rack. He set the half-empty plate of scones on the middle rack.

He nodded at their thanks and turned away.

Krista nudged her teacup and saucer to the side. While the others served up the sandwiches, she poured her tea. The dark golden color still seemed anemic to her, but it would have to do.

Lacey had taken only two offerings, but Merci loaded her plate with one of each.

"I'll pass on the salmon." Krista wrinkled her nose as she placed the cucumber and chicken salad finger sandwiches onto her plate.

"You should really take a small taste," Lacey said.

Merci bit into the fish topped cracker.

Krista blew on her tea, awaiting her niece's verdict.

"Not overly salty like most smoked fish." She took another bite and Krista sipped her tea.

Hot. A mellow blend of flavors she would have identified as tea-like tingled over her tongue. Not bad. For tea.

Merci polished off the salmon. "I'd eat another before deciding I didn't like it." She grinned, keeping her lips closed, and then raised her teacup toward Krista.

"I'll keep that in mind," Krista muttered.

"This chicken salad is divine." Lacey dabbed at her lips with a napkin. "The curried onions are amazing."

Curry? Krista plucked the sandwich up and nibbled on it. Flavor exploded in her mouth, and the hint of spice didn't overpower the chicken and dressing.

Comments interspersed with slow tastes of each fancy sandwich. After a small nibble, Krista passed her salmon to Merci, agreeing it wasn't salty but still too fishy for her tastes. In the end, she loved the beef sandwich best, a surprise since pickled red onions weren't on her list of favorite things.

After stating she liked the tartlet best, Merci added, "Grandma would have chosen the cucumber sandwich."

Krista glanced toward the empty chair, almost expecting her mother to chime in with a yea or nay to Merci's declaration.

"She would have been a fan of the dill cream cheese

spread on dark rye," Lacey agreed, avoiding eye contact with Krista while glancing toward the vacant seat.

Did she feel Mom's presence, too?

"The fennel was a bit much for me," Krista said, "but Mom did adore her all-vegetable sandwiches."

Merci shivered. "I remember when she tried to feed me an onion sandwich."

Krista's lips tilted up. Onion, tomato, and cucumber had been harvested from their garden, sliced, and made into sandwiches. She preferred meat with her tomato and had happily passed on the other vegetables.

"It's not as bad as you might think," Lacey said, staring into her teacup after making the ridiculous claim.

Krista and Merci made noises of disgust. Lacey frowned at them.

"If you didn't try it, you can't say one way or another."

"I can! Onions are disgusting." Merci rapped her palm on the table, jangling the silver and china.

"I don't need to eat dirt to know I don't like it." Krista raised her chin as Lacey rolled her eyes.

A warm sensation of approval swelled from beside her. Mom chuckling? Krista could almost hear it. The dark shadow that had fallen over her on that January day lightened.

Neatly dressed servers swarmed the room to disperse a plate of treats to each table. The plate had barely settled onto the silver serving tower when their waiter cleared his throat and pointed out each item before offering to answer questions.

"Which should I try first?" Merci's rapt attention implied the answer carried great weight.

"The cranberry shortbread is the perfect marriage

between sweet and tart," he said. "How is everyone doing with tea?"

"I could use a hot pot," Lacey said.

After Krista and Merci claimed they were fine, the waiter nodded and slipped away.

Krista poured a second cup while Lacey and Merci served themselves from the top rack. Merci took three items, including the cranberry shortbread. Krista didn't curl her lip but even the waiter's poetic description didn't inspire any interest. Lacey took a tart and mousse cup.

Krista inhaled the sweet scent of the desserts and nestled her shoulders into the chair while sipping the warm tea. The mellow taste heightened the food's flavors.

"This red velvet with candied citrus. Amazing." Merci drew the last word out for four syllables.

Krista's mouth twitched into a slight smile. An aura of contentment encircled their table. She glanced at the empty chair, narrowing her eyes to imagine Mom sitting there. The picture came easily, and the lump rising in her throat felt more like happiness at the company than sadness over loss.

"You'll want that Almond Florentine," Lacey said in her usual bossy, big sister voice.

"Dark chocolate and almonds. I'm in." Krista took the two chocolate items and at the last moment slid the mousse onto her last clean plate.

"The mousse is divine." Lacey set her spoon on the plate and patted her stomach. "I don't think we'll need dinner tonight."

Merci giggled. "You might be right, but I reserve the right to change my mind in a few hours."

The caramelized almonds flaked as Krista cut into them and savored the first bite. The bittersweet chocolate melted into the almonds, dissolving on her tongue in a burst of rich flavor.

"And?" Lacey asked.

"You can have my serving of red velvet in exchange for your Almond Florentine."

Lacey shook her head. "You're not the only dark chocolate lover around here."

"I'll take your red velvet, Aunt K. And you can have my almond thingy. I prefer milk chocolate."

Merci scraped the lovely dark chocolate pastry onto Krista's plate and snagged the red velvet from the tray.

With sweet teeth satisfied, the trio relaxed with fresh cups of tea in hand.

"What dessert do you think Grandma would have liked best?"

Krista opened her mouth and closed it, sipping tea instead. Lacey should answer first this time.

"Maybe the tart," Lacey said after a few beats of silence. "But she hadn't eaten much chocolate in several years, so maybe the banana caramel mousse."

"She loved chocolate, though," Krista murmured, staring into her teacup.

"I hope she's eating her fill of it in Heaven," Merci said. "I was going to vote for the banana. Her banana pudding was the best, but this leveled it up with the caramel."

The cake had surprised Krista. She'd planned to scrape the mousse off the top but had taken a small taste of both layers together. The three flavors melded well, minimizing the overpowering taste of bananas.

"She would have liked all of them," Krista said. Merci shook her head at the non-answer. "Her sweet tooth was famous, and she rarely met a dessert she didn't like."

"I think you mean infamous," Lacey said, a small smile creasing her face. "Ice cream swayed her every single time."

Krista recalled the endless stream of ice cream cartons that had followed the first round of chemotherapy. Mom couldn't hold down much else, so the doctor had cleared her to have three meals of ice cream daily, as long as she ate the natural kind without all the chemical additives that fattened cancer cells.

"It almost made the chemotherapy worth it," Krista said. The other two stared at her with wide eyes. She cocked her head. "That's what Mom told me."

"I can hear her saying that," Merci said. "Is the worst thing about cancer that you know it's killing you?" Merci tapped her short fingernails on the handle of her fork. "Or that it makes you give up living before it kills you?"

"What does that even mean?" Lacey furrowed her brow.

Krista pursed her lips but felt a nudge from the presence beside her. "Mom had to give up chocolate and sweets which she loved. So, was she still living?"

Lacey stiffened. "Life is about more than food."

Merci rolled her eyes. "Of course it is, Mom. That's not the point. Life is supposed to be about enjoyment, living in the moment, savoring all the things." She took another bite of dessert to punctuate her statement.

"Like chocolate." Krista watched her sister, waiting for understanding to dawn.

"And travel." Merci twisted to stare at her mother.

The fork dangled as Lacey stopped chewing. "Because chemo destroyed her taste buds, I didn't think she missed those foods." She swallowed as her eyes misted. "But I've missed them."

"She missed them." Merci patted her mother's arm. "But

you can taste them, Mom, and you should. It doesn't have to be dessert every meal."

"Or even every day," Krista agreed, heart jumping at the thought of treating herself instead of overindulging to soothe her wayward emotions. "But when we do eat the dessert," she raised the sliver of Almond Florentine on her fork as if in salute, "we should fully enjoy it. No regrets."

Merci raised her spoonful of mousse. "No regrets."

Lacey's gaze darted toward the empty chair before she straightened and raised her bite of red velvet. "No regrets. I hope Mom had no regrets."

No regrets. It should have been a sobering thought. But the tang of chocolate and almonds reminded Krista this snapshot moment wouldn't be repeated and could never be duplicated. She swallowed the rich dessert. A brush against her arm raised the hair there.

Lacey dropped her gaze and dabbed at her eyes with her napkin.

"She would have loved every moment of this," her sister said, soft words nearly lost in the clink of china and silver from nearby diners.

"I think she did." Krista stared pointedly at the seat beside her. "Didn't you feel her approval?"

"I thought I was the only one." Tears added the sparkle of diamonds to Merci's hazel eyes.

Krista smiled at her niece, hoping to waylay the rising moisture intent on smearing her mascara.

"She was in the rose garden, too," Lacey whispered.

Krista imagined it would have been a perfect place for Mom's spirit to connect with her sister. "You two loved working with those rose bushes."

Merci wrinkled her nose. "I preferred clipping off the

pretty blooms for indoor bouquets."

"Your aunt wouldn't be caught near the garden for anything." Lacey's rueful tone held no unkindness or condemnation.

"My black thumb wasn't welcome." Krista shrugged and swallowed a mouthful of tepid tea. A little ice, and it would hit the spot.

More jibes and laughter floated around the table. Lacey's gaze lingered on the empty place, the napkin still folded neatly beside the stacked dishes and the waiting teacup. While her sister's green eyes sparkled, Krista's heart tapped in excitement, knowing her sister felt Mom's presence, too.

Thank you, Lord, for letting her take tea with us.

For the first time since that horrible day in January, peace reigned in every corner of Krista's heart, mind, and soul. This might only be a baby step on the path to reconciliation, but it made Krista's feet tap out a victory dance.

Conversation or Confrontation?

To Lacey Bloom, an emotional conversation and a hand grenade were the same thing. Which is why she avoided those types of talks. Her stomach knotted as she pulled open the bedroom door. She wanted to hide in the room as she'd done every other night of the trip, but an invisible presence prodded her forward.

To face the firing squad? That's what it felt like.

Everything had seemed possible in the tearoom. With every glance toward the empty seat, confirmation of her mother's approval chimed in her heart. A halo of light wrapped the fancy chair for most of the afternoon. She wished the shared camaraderie could be worn like the lovely hat Mom had supplied for the event.

But she couldn't stay in the fancy tearoom, the same way she hadn't been able to remain in the garden. At least its peace had burrowed deeply into her heart.

Those hours sharing tea had reminded her of the companionship and acceptance she'd been missing since the problems with her sister had escalated. Why was she holding the door to reconciliation closed? Several times during the week, Krista had asked with uneasy tentativeness about the wall between them. Last night, she'd tried to join Lacey for her after dinner walk, but Lacey had pretended not to hear and rushed away. She hadn't wanted to revisit those painful moments.

She still wasn't prepared to confront them. Might never be ready. But today, she'd break her silence.

A gnawing anxiety sucked her stomach toward her feet. What if nothing changed?

The whispers of doubt made her pause on the threshold. Avoiding hard things had become her safe space.

She sensed that Mom wanted her to face this conversation head-on. Lacey had spent enough time dodging her sister's weak attempts to communicate.

She willed her spine into steel and stepped into the vacant main room. Movement in her peripheral vision jerked her attention toward the balcony where Krista stood.

Whispering a plea for help directed at she didn't know who, Lacey pushed open the outer door. A gust of sea air filled with squawking gulls battered her reluctance.

Krista faced the harbor and said, "It was more than amazing."

Lacey twisted to stare and spied the phone at her sister's ear. She'd be talking to her husband. Again.

A vile reptile curled in the hollow of Lacey's chest. Jealousy. Another emotion that built bricks in the wall of isolation. She sighed and imagined nudging the snake off the ledge near her sister's bare feet.

Goodbye, envy. I'm happy my sister has a wonderful marriage.

With a start, she realized the statement wasn't exactly

true. Seeds of resentment had been planted in her heart when Todd offered his wife and sons so many things Lacey had never had with Grant. Over the years, she had ignored the feelings, but everyone knew weeds didn't need special care to flourish.

Krista turned and stiffened slightly before holding up one finger. "I'm sure you managed fine," she said into the phone.

Lacey ducked inside and paced toward the padded armchair closest to the dining table. She'd claimed it the day they arrived. Sitting there meant, when they were all together, that she forced Merci and Krista to share the narrow sofa.

Lacey rubbed her thumb across the logo on her water bottle—the symbol of crossed weights Evan had chosen for Holmes Gym. She hadn't thought of work in a few days. An amazing feat since it had ranked supreme in her thoughts since January. How had her classes at the gym gone? Had Evan been able to reschedule her private sessions?

Krista pushed through the door, a tentative smile turning up her glossy pink lips.

"The boys think they're starving on barbecue and takeout." Her laugh rang false, a gong instead of a cymbal. She shook her head. "As if."

"When do they head back to college?" Kids, a safe topic.

"Two weeks for Jon and still a month for Hunter. It sure will be quiet once they're gone."

Lacey knew all about quiet. Maybe that was the main reason she spent so much time at the gym. Even when she wasn't working.

Krista settled on the far end of the couch and placed her phone face down on the black-topped coffee table.

"Where's Merci?"

"Making a call."

"Stephan, no doubt." Krista's eyes sparkled. "Ah, young love."

Lacey stiffened. What did she know about love? The longer she lived, the more she understood how little she knew about most things. Was her daughter falling in love?

Ugly envy squeezed inside her. After briefly considering when she'd become so jealous about everything, she banished the unwelcome emotion.

"You think they're in love?" Lacey worried the idea in her mind.

Stephan lived in California. He'd seemed nice enough when she'd met him at graduation the previous year, but surely a long-distance relationship couldn't survive.

"It seems likely. She's talked to him more than I've spoken to my husband." Krista smirked. "More than friends would talk when one of them is on the vacation of a lifetime."

It had been the vacation of a lifetime. Lacey stared toward the windows and let a replay of the highlights flit through her mind. The castle. The schoolhouse. The beautiful roses. Fragrant tea and scrumptious goodies.

Thank you, Mom. This trip was everything you promised.

Thoughts of Mom redirected her from the urge to ponder Merci's love life. That's not the conversation she needed to have today. Lacey pushed her spine into the cushion and inhaled long and deep, as if preparing to dive in and swim the length of the pool. Which—in a metaphorical sense—she was.

"I'm glad she's not here. We need to talk."

Krista flinched. Her hands curled together in her lap

while she kept her blue-gray stare fixed on Lacey.

Lacey searched for the perfect way to start something she'd avoided for months and dreaded all week. Best just to say it.

"You hurt me," she blurted.

Krista's head flew back as if the words were a physical slap.

"I needed you when the church dumped me, and Grant did everything he could to destroy my life." The bitter words flowed. "But you were too busy with your perfect job and family, burying yourself in getting a degree you don't need."

A pang jabbed her chest. That wasn't fair. She knew her sister had dreamed of being a teacher since childhood.

"I lost everything." Krista opened her mouth, and Lacey held up her hand. "I appreciate that you gave me a place to stay that first month, but once I moved to Castle Rock it was as if...as if...I fell off the face of the earth."

Krista blinked. Probably fighting tears.

Lacey glanced toward the windows. Now that she'd opened the floodgates, she wouldn't allow her sister's tears to stop this.

"Talking on the phone was fine, but I was alone. None of my friends would return my calls. It was like I had a limb amputated."

Before the divorce, Lacey had invested herself in being a mother and working at the church. The divorce neatly severed her from both roles. Motherhood had been changing since Merci left for college, and Lucas had withdrawn from her as his friends and activities filled most of his time. But suddenly not seeing her son daily felt like banishment.

Grant couldn't stop her from seeing Lucas since their

no-contest divorce didn't address custody or marital support, but he had made it difficult. He'd bribed Lucas with cash for computer games and gas for the hand-me-down truck her son drove.

And church? Grant had spread lies, and the people she'd worked side-by-side with for years believed them. While her husband attended on holidays or for special events, she'd rarely missed a regular service and had spent hours organizing activities to grow their Sunday school program. It made zero sense for them to take his side, but so little had made sense this past year.

To cope with the vacancy in her life, she'd taken on more hours at the gym and finally started the nutritionist certification program at the community college, but those were activities, not relationships.

"Where were you, Krista?"

Her sister blinked rapidly. "I should have been there. But you stopped returning my calls—"

"You weren't listening to what I needed. And I was sick of begging for my best friend to understand me."

Krista swallowed. "You're right. I was too caught up in my own life."

Lacey shook her head, not ready to hear an apology.

"When mom needed to go for regular treatments, I wanted to help. But I *have to* work. And you?" She shook her head. "You could have eased the burden on Dad, but you used going to school as an excuse. I know hospitals make you uncomfortable, but life is full of uncomfortable things."

Krista's voice was small. "I took her that last time."

"Once. You took her one time because Dad wasn't feeling well that day." The spill of words drained the well of anger. Hollowness echoed in the chasm of grief she'd been forging a bridge across all week. Maybe she'd held on to the fury for so long because that was easier to face than loneliness and loss.

"I'm sorry." Tears thickened Krista's voice. "I should have done more. I did need to student teach, but the program director and Mrs. Curry offered to lighten my schedule those last few weeks." She wiped her cheek.

"See? The program director had more influence with you than your family."

"But I didn't want to be there. I hated seeing her like that." Krista drew a shaky breath. "That wasn't Mom."

A picture of their mother's emaciated form in the hospital bed filled Lacey's mind. Yes, that wasn't how Mom had been in life, but that didn't mean she should be abandoned during her final days.

"You were there for her final moments." A wave of regret propelled the words. "I spent days with her, but the daughter who hadn't been there got that final hour. It's so unfair."

On a whoosh of air, Krista said, "I would gladly have changed places with you."

Those words fanned flames of indignation. "See? You're ungrateful for the precious things. Oh, it was too painful to hear her labored breaths. Selfish."

Krista's red-rimmed eyes poured in streams. She nodded, and that movement stalled the tirade flowing from Lacey's mouth. She hadn't expected agreement.

"I am. I worked and went to school." She pursed her lips. "Because I needed to stay busy."

"Stay in denial, you mean." Lacey had spent enough time there to know all about it.

"Maybe. But in the end, it didn't matter. You know why?

Because I prayed for God to take her." Her voice broke. "I prayed for Mom to die. And then...then..."

She stumbled toward the box of tissues sitting on the shelf beneath the television. She yanked a couple free, mopped her face, and blew her nose.

Determination laced with guilt framed her next words. "After she was gone, I felt relieved. Only the worst daughter in the world prays for her mother to die and then is glad when the prayer is answered."

Lacey gaped. Every thought she'd had, every recounting of her sister's many failures over the past eighteen months blinked out. Horror welled. This was the guilt her sister carried?

Lacey would have prayed for Mom's suffering to be relieved. If she'd still believed in God. And, truthfully, when she'd gotten that message...

"Your text."

Krista covered her mouth and shook her head. "I'm so, so sorry about that. One of the teachers I worked with got a text from her brother saying their mother had died, and I thought that was the coldest way to deliver the news." Krista blew her nose again. "Even though I could hardly talk, I should have called you. I'm sorry I didn't."

Lacey's stomach and heart collided. It was easy to imagine her sister as a sobbing mess. Lacey had sat in the bank parking lot after reading the text, face buried in her arms, unable to drive anywhere for at least twenty minutes.

"When I got your text, I was mad at myself for not being there." So much anger. "Nursing the hurt and stewing on it has been a way to feel something other than devastation." Lacey's leg twitched. She should hug her sister. Wanted to. "When I read the text, I felt relieved, too."

Shame swept across her, but she released it on a forced exhalation. Once Mom had breathed her last breath, she'd gone to a better place. No matter how much God had let Lacey down, she knew he had welcomed her mother into Heaven with open arms.

Let you down? A voice she remembered from the garden spoke into her heart. *Did you come to me?*

Silence splintered into shards that pierced Lacey's broken heart. Because she hadn't turned to God. When people in church had betrayed her, she'd accepted it without a fight. Within weeks, she'd stopped reading her Bible or praying. Mom had encouraged her to attend services with them, but Lacey didn't want to. She hadn't been able to face people she'd known her entire life, certain they were judging her failures.

Let the one without sin judge. Maybe that thought was a scripture. Maybe not. But it cut into Lacey's softening heart. Hadn't she been judging her sister all these months?

"Todd says relief is a natural part of grief," Krista murmured. "But it felt wrong. And it's clear I made the wrong things a priority."

Lacey squinted. What did she mean?

"Why wouldn't we feel relieved, K? Mom's pain and suffering were over." She gulped. "She's happy now, right?"

Too bad that assurance felt like an empty platitude to Lacey's lonely heart. But sometimes, truth hurt. And other times the truth sounded like a lie, especially when it wasn't what a person wanted to hear.

"You're right. I wasn't there for you or Dad. I made getting a degree my priority." Krista dabbed at her red eyes. "And what do I have to show for it?"

Lacey blinked. The question swiped her list of

151

accusations from her mind. She hadn't considered her sister's life to be missing anything. Krista had a loving husband, beautiful home, strong church family, and means to pursue her dreams. Except getting a degree wasn't the dream.

"People at church warned me that I had the wrong priorities." Krista's voice hardened, as if she was parroting those people. "They said I should delay my student teaching and put school on hold when Mom went in the hospital that last time."

The hospital stay that involved singing carols over an Internet connection on Christmas Eve. Lacey swallowed hard and blinked at the sting of tears. Her sister was admitting her faults. Isn't this what she wanted to hear?

"But I didn't do it. I wanted to stay busy, so I didn't have to think about the fact that—" Tears choked off her words.

"Mom was dying." Their mother. Lacey witnessed the pain in her sister's expression and sagging shoulders, but she'd imagined Krista hadn't been as broken by the loss as her. After all, people rallied around Krista, while Lacey struggled alone.

But grieving was a solitary venture. No one could ease it or speed it. Lacey had tried to explain that when Lucas said he didn't want to talk about Grandma because it made him want to cry. He didn't believe her because she had refused to cry in front of anyone, choosing to wear the facade of strength she believed everyone needed to see.

Krista stared until Lacey met her gaze. "Thank you for being there for her, Lace." She wiped her nose. "I couldn't handle it, but you managed everything so well. I should have told you that before."

Tenderness swept into the dark places death had carved

in Lacey's soul. Her efforts to be there for Mom had been appreciated. Those days would have been stressful if a bunch of people had camped out at the house, so why had Lacey expected Krista to be there all the time?

Inside Lacey's chest, something crumbled. An avalanche pounded her lungs and stomach while tears rolled and she sobbed. She gasped for breath as the emotional tidal wave thrashed her soul.

"Oh, Lace." Krista trotted across the room and knelt in front of Lacey, squeezing her knee. Her sister whispered something Lacey couldn't make out over her own blubbering.

She wanted to stop. But the dam of emotions wouldn't be denied its release. Grief, anger, fear, anxiety, and more bubbled to the surface and flowed outward. A hollow, empty room opened in her heart, waiting to be filled with something new.

"Heal us. Please, Jesus." Krista's words penetrated once the gut-wrenching upheaval ceased.

Warmth swelled through the vacancy inside Lacey. Someone had prayed for her, and the lightheaded, nearly out-of-body sensation made it clear that God was answering. God who had allowed her to feel Mom's presence among the roses. God who had pursued her in the garden until she admitted she shared the blame for the rift with her sister.

I'm sorry, Lord. I don't know if I deserve healing, but I want it.

She took a shuddering breath, and a loud squeak came with it. Krista stayed beside her, lips moving with silent words. More prayers.

A breeze swept over her arm as Merci arrived beside her chair. "Everything okay out here?"

Lacey swiveled toward her. "We're getting things out in the open."

Krista rose and dropped a box of tissues on Lacey's chair.

Taking two, Lacey wiped her eyes and blew her nose. At the sound of her sister doing the same, a smile twitched at the corners of her lips. How was it possible she felt like smiling?

The tumult inside stilled, and a strange blanket descended, like snow drifting to cover the dead winter landscape.

"I feel strange."

"Is this the first time you've cried since Grandma died?" Merci scooted back to sit on her heels.

"No, but it's the first time I've wept. Ever." Which seemed strange when Lacey had lost so much in the past couple of years.

"You feel empty," Krista said, "in a good way."

Lacey's head bobbed. Another breeze whispered behind her, like fingertips stroking the back of her neck.

Mom, is this what you wanted?

A ray of sunshine burst through the cloudy day in Lacey's heart. She pictured Mom smiling down from Heaven.

And Lacey suddenly wondered why she'd been avoiding this conversation with her sister for so many months. Especially since Mom had tried to get her to open up about it and make things right.

"It will help you in ways you can't imagine," Mom had told her after everyone else had left on her birthday.

Mom was right. As always. Lacey leaned back in the chair and basked in the sense that now she was right, too.

Spilling the Secret

I must be royalty. Mercedes Bloom grinned at the thought. Stuffed with special pastries, she couldn't imagine a more perfect afternoon. Well, maybe if she hadn't needed to wear cute sandals that pinched her feet.

After sinking onto one of the twin beds in her room at the condo she shared with her mom and aunt, Merci massaged her feet. She groaned as her fingers kneaded out the knots her stylish shoes had caused.

Surprisingly, she hadn't felt sad during the tea. Instead, Merci had sensed a closeness with Grandma. Best of all, her mom and Aunt K had connected, almost like the old days when they were best friends.

Would Grandma get her wish?

Merci snuck toward her door and cracked it open. The drone of voices drifted from the main room. Her heart lightened. It finally seemed like Mom and Aunt K were talking things out.

She crossed her fingers and stared at the ceiling. *It's*

happening.

Merci pulled out her phone and dropped a photo from the tea in the IM chat thread she shared with Stephan. He'd still be at his parents' store, but maybe business would be slow, and he'd have time to chat.

Merci tossed her empty suitcase onto the end of the other bed and sighed. Packing to go home was the worst part of any vacation.

Her phone vibrated with a response notification. *Looks posh. Go good?*

Stephan and his short answers. Merci plopped on the edge of the bed and gave him the highlights. Anyone who wanted a taste of royal treatment should take high tea.

After sending her lengthy message, Merci flipped open the suitcase. The video call chime sounded before she made her way to the dresser beneath the window.

She grinned and accepted the call. Since they'd resorted to voice calls this week instead of their usual video chats, she'd missed seeing Stephan's handsome face. Merci hoped the resort's Wi-Fi could handle the call without lagging.

"Hey," she said, scooting back against the padded headboard of the empty bed.

His face blurred into view. "But how did it go?"

"Perfect. They're in the living room talking now."

He nodded. "And your mom is still okay about you quitting school?"

Merci shook her head. "Not okay exactly. But she's not nagging me."

"Things went better than you thought. I've been praying for you."

"So you said." She drew the phone closer. "Thanks. It made a difference."

"You made a difference. Grandma would be proud."

Warmth seeped into her arms, almost like Grandma hugged her from behind. It wasn't the first time she'd felt Grandma's presence on this trip. And she hoped she'd continue to sense that closeness after returning home.

Voices raised beyond her mostly closed door. Merci's heart vaulted into her throat as she sprang to her feet.

"Uh oh. Things are getting loud out there."

"Time to insert your calming presence into the situation?"

Merci nodded her head. He had such confidence in her. "Pray?"

"Always."

They ended the call. Merci shoved open her bedroom door and tripped down the short hallway.

Aunt Krista, tears pouring down a puffy red face, knelt in front of the chair where her mother sat. Weeping. Had Merci seen her mother cry since Grandma's funeral? It had to be a good sign, didn't it?

"Everything okay out here?"

Her mother swiveled toward her. "We're getting things out in the open."

Which is what Grandma wanted. But by the looks on their faces, it seemed as if Aunt K had done all the soul-bearing and Mom hadn't quite forgiven her. How could she remind them they needed each other?

Tell them. Grandma's voice whispered in her ear. *No more secrets.*

Merci's gut clenched. Her gaze darted between her aunt and mother. Aunt K grabbed a tissue box from beside the television and set it on the arm of Mom's chair. She shuffled to the fireplace and faced the window while blowing her nose. Tension blanketed the room.

Merci wondered how would telling her secrets help.

It would shock them. And they would react like mothers, which would place them on the same side of the issue. Dizziness shook Merci, and she stumbled toward the wall.

Oh, Jesus. Is this really what needs to happen?

No one spoke. Currents of emotion weighted the silence.

Merci swallowed before blurting, "I'm moving."

Lacey gasped and Krista whirled to face them.

Merci clenched her hands and marched into the center of the room. Might as well face the firing squad with fake confidence. "I gave my notice before I came. I'll work two more weeks after we get home."

"Gave your notice? How will you pay your student loans?" Mom gaped at her from the chair.

"Moving?" her aunt stepped closer. "Out of your apartment?"

Merci nodded. "Moving to California."

The words fell like a rock into a still pool. Aunt K shuffled zombie-like to the edge of the couch closest to Mom and crumpled onto the cushion.

"Stephan invited me. He wants to take our relationship to the next level."

"You're moving in with Stephan?" her mom nearly shrieked.

Merci shook her head. A dagger pricked her heart. She'd never accepted the rumors that her mom had been unfaithful, but that's the first thing she thought of Merci?

"I'll stay with his parents and work in their shop. He's been offered a full-time position at his church."

"Doesn't he live with his parents?" Her mom's hands

clenched together in her lap.

Merci shrugged. "Yeah, but they're devout Orthodox. We won't be sharing a room. Is that what you thought?"

Mom recoiled and shook her head.

"Wow. That's a big step." Krista glanced toward Mom. "Did he propose? Is that why you're moving there?"

Merci sank onto the other end of the sofa. Her head drooped. "He loves me. Marriage is the next step, but he wants to court me." It sounded so old-fashioned. Butterflies swarmed her stomach at the thought. "It's a little difficult when we live in different states."

"Don't give up everything for a man." Mom sagged back in her seat. "You'll regret it."

Merci squinted at her mother. She ground her back teeth, keeping angry words from spilling out. *I'm not you. Stephan isn't Dad. Let me figure out my own life.*

"What she means—" Aunt Krista took a swig of water and rested her elbows on her knees. "Don't sell all your stuff and move to a different state without a backup plan."

"That's not—" Her mom hiccupped. "A bad idea." Her gaping jaws and startled eyes made it clear she'd intended to say something different.

Merci pressed her lips in a line to keep her grin from escaping, and her churning belly settled. It was working. They were on the same side.

"What about a job?" Aunt Krista's face wore an open, accepting expression.

"There's a possibility of a position with the church where he's the music minister." Merci pursed her lips together. "It would only be part-time."

"What kind of position?" Her mother sounded skeptical.

The honest conversation with her mother thawed

something in the crevice within Merci created by her parents' divorce. For years before it had happened, she'd watched her mom shrink into herself, battered by Dad's constant criticism. When Mom had called to say she'd left him, Merci had felt relieved because she hated to see her parents unhappy. Since then, a barrier had formed between her and Mom, a line she couldn't cross without feeling like she was choosing a side. And because of that, they hadn't had deep conversations anymore.

"Women's and Children's ministries. Finding and designing curriculum, scheduling, directing teachers."

Both of them were nodding.

"Sounds perfect." Aunt K smiled.

Her mom crossed her arms. "But part-time won't pay your bills."

Not this again. Why did everything have to be about money?

"I'll figure it out."

Her mother paled and her breathing sounded harsh. Merci leaned forward.

"Mom? Are you okay?"

Her mother shook her head. "Of course not. I don't want you to move away." She stiffened. "What if things don't work out? You're giving up everything for a man."

"Am I? Stephan is the only thing I'm sure about right now." Merci sighed. "I have to do this."

More silence. Merci could see her mother trying to keep her emotions under wraps. Mom had suffered so much loss in the past two years. Merci didn't want to cause her more pain. But it was time for all of them to start living again, and for Merci, that meant probing deeper into her love for Stephan.

"Well, it's obvious you two love each other." Krista smiled. "And you're willing to do the work. Those are two ingredients for a successful relationship."

"It's pretty scary. But I can't imagine life without him."

"I can't lose you, too," Mom choked out. Tears trickled down one side of her face, and her lips trembled.

Merci hopped to her feet and crouched beside Mom's chair. Her hands felt hot against Mom's chill ones as she laced her fingers through her mother's as she used to do in childhood.

Aunt K knelt at Mom's other side, hand on her shoulder with a watery, empathetic gaze fixed on Mom's face.

"You're not losing me. It's just a visit." Although she knew if Stephan had anything to say about it, Merci wouldn't return to Oregon without him.

"Don't make your life about him. That's all I ask." Her mother's voice wavered.

"Stephan loves God, Mom. And he supports my decisions." Merci bit back the rest of the words she wanted to say. Things about her father and how Stephan was nothing like him. But that would be vaulting over the line she'd drawn to keep from being caught between her parents.

"But you've given up on your career dreams."

Merci blew out a frustrated breath. "I don't know what I want to do for a career. Big deal. I know I want to be with Stephan."

"But California? What if it doesn't work out?" Mom gulped back tears and straightened, her sudden show of grief disappearing.

"What if it does?" Aunt K inserted.

Mom's head jerked toward Aunt K.

"If Stephan is the right man and this is the right time for

them to be together, I'm happy for Merci." She patted Mom's shoulder. "Surely you don't want Merci to never fall in love, get married, or have kids."

Mom blinked and sucked in a breath. "I want her to have all those things…when the time is right. But I don't want her to give up her career aspirations to do it."

"I don't know what I want to do, Mom. And when I do, I know Stephan will support me one hundred percent."

"And it's never too late to go back to school," Aunt K said, nudging Mom's shoulder.

Mom pursed her lips but nodded slowly. "I'll miss you so much."

Merci leaned forward. Mom met her halfway and they hugged. Her mother's arms squeezed her sides, and Merci nestled her face into Mom's neck. The scent of peaches swirled through Merci's senses.

"Who's ready to plan a wedding?" Aunt K grinned.

Mom stiffened and swatted at her sister. Aunt K sidled backward, bumping the sofa before rising up to sit on it.

Laughter burst from Merci's tight lungs.

"Whoa now." She shook her head. "He hasn't actually proposed."

"And there's no rush," Mom said firmly.

Warmth swirled between Merci's heart and cheeks. Her mother and aunt shared a calm, knowing look. The stifling tarp of tension blew away, and a thin sheet of relief settled over the room.

Somewhere, hovering above them, Grandma was smiling. Merci knew it.

"How about a game a cribbage?" She pushed to her feet.

Aunt K said, "Sure" at the same time Mom said, "Sounds fine."

The three shared a wide-eyed look. Merci grinned, while the others shook their heads.

"Prepare to lose," Merci said, trotting back to her room to retrieve the cards and game board from the top of her dresser.

Not that it was possible. She had a sense they had all become winners today.

Who knew spilling her secrets would be what tipped the scales in favor of reconciliation?

Grandma. And God.

An unexpected benefit came in the form of lightheartedness. Merci hadn't realized the weight those secrets had put on her mind and heart.

With her hands on the knob to her room, Merci tilted her face toward the ceiling.

"Thanks," she whispered, and shared another satisfied smile with Grandma.

A Promised Plan

The Final Answer

Wind tossed Krista White's shoulder length tresses against her cheeks while she leaned against the rail of the ferry's upper deck. The wake bubbled behind the southward bound ferry heading back to the United States, home, and reality.

She wanted to hold tightly to the peace of sensing Mom's approval in the tearoom and the joy of reconciliation with her sister. But once she got home, life would interfere again. Maybe her sister was right, and she should quit her job at the credit union and get on the substitute teacher list for the local school district. But that was a decision for tomorrow.

Today, she stood beside her fellow travelers, watching the ferry pull out of the harbor. Soon, Victoria was a blip at the horizon behind them. Ruffled water stretched in every direction.

Merci hip-bumped her mother. "I'm going to find some shade."

"Good idea," Lacey said.

With her pale skin, Merci spent most of her outdoor time in the shade or at least shaded by a large-brimmed hat.

A memory flashed in Krista's mind. Her mother, Lacey, and Merci wore matching hats at a Mother's Day tea hosted by their church years ago. Emotion swelled in her throat, but she choked it down and faced her sister.

"I wish I could change things." The words made her stomach dip.

Lacey pulled her gaze from a pair of diving gulls. Her green eyes nearly matched the water in color. "I could have asked for help. But there's no going back."

Krista wished that wasn't true. The sisters had been best friends for two decades, so close they could read each other's thoughts and feelings without words. Krista had known Lacey was suffering loneliness and struggling with changes. She should have checked in with her sister more often, but she'd let her drive to graduate at the top of her college class dominate her life.

"I put school above everything. And look where that got me."

Krista had accepted assurances from her parents and mutual friends that Lacey was adjusting to single life, but working all the time didn't replace the fellowship of a church family. Lacey's life had imploded after the divorce, and Krista should have reached out and helped her sister.

Especially since Krista knew Lacey had always struggled to ask for help, believing it was a sign of weakness. Krista understood because she battled that, too. It was a character trait they shared with their mother.

Lacey squeezed her forearm. "School is hard for old ladies."

Lacey tilted her face toward the sunshine, her relaxed pose completely opposite from what it had been the last time they'd ridden this ferry. Was it really only a week ago? So much had happened, making it seem like a month had passed.

"Not as hard as funerals." Krista gasped in realization. "The funeral! So many of them were there. Did they…" She couldn't bear to finish the thought. That day had required Herculean emotional stamina for everyone, but only Lacey'd had to face people who mistreated and misjudged her.

Lacey pursed her lips. "I'd rather not think about it. They gave the usual responses."

I'm praying for you. Your mother was such an inspiration. She's in a better place. Oh, Krista could recite a list of inanities. She'd spewed some of them at funerals herself. But never again. A hug spoke more than a thousand words ever could, and that was all she planned to offer in the future.

"It still floors me that every one of your friends from church dropped you like a hot potato." Krista shook her head at the audacity. "As if you would have an affair. Ridiculous!"

"None of them knew about Grant's manipulative side. He's played them all." Lacey's lips quirked. "And hasn't been back to church since Christmas, according to Lucas."

Krista's heart ached. Her sister had been placed on the outside of so many things. With Merci moving to California, she'd only have Lucas. While Krista loved the relationship she shared with her adult sons, it was nothing like the bond of mother and daughter. Add to that Grant's controlling nature. Krista bet he would work overtime to keep Lucas from hanging out with his mom. She could almost hear him saying, *Possession is nine-tenths of the law.*

"I can't believe Lucas is a senior." Time flowed swiftly and didn't offer second chances. Krista's sons were both in college, but their elementary school days seemed only a year or two in the past.

"He has an appointment for senior pictures next week." The wind whipped the sigh from Lacey's lips. "Grant doesn't think he needs anything except what the school provides for ID cards, so I'll have to find a way to pay for them." Her shoulders sagged.

"Men." Krista paused to consider whether her next words might be well-received.

Lord, I want to help my sister. Soften her heart.

"You know," she finally said, "most people would gladly pay for their copies of his pictures. And we could help with the initial deposit."

Lacey scowled. "I can figure it out."

Krista nodded. "No doubt. But we all want senior pictures of Lucas and don't mind paying for them."

Air rushed past. Murmurs and shuffles of other passengers roared in the silence between them.

Lord, please. Help Lacey release her pride in the area of finances.

Lacey sighed. "I'll think about it."

Krista nodded. That was a baby step in the right direction, and she needed to take one of her own by getting time with her sister on their calendar. If she didn't, life might get in the way, and she wasn't willing to risk backsliding.

"Do you think we could have lunch next weekend? And I'd like to get back to weekly calls, too."

Lacey blinked. "I teach on Saturday mornings."

"What time do you finish? I can bring something to the gym if that's what we need to do."

Lacey cocked her head and furrowed her brow. On the railing, their reddish-brown arms could have been twins. Krista had missed her sister. And for what? Not to land a dream job.

Guilt clawed from somewhere. Apparently, she hadn't banished it completely. On its heels came disappointment, but she felt no sting. Time rolled on, and she didn't want to forget one of the lessons Mom's passing had taught her: relationships should be prioritized over career.

Lord, forgive me for failing my mother, father, and sister. Help me be there for Lacey and Dad now.

The pain gripping Krista's chest eased until the breeze seemed to carry it away. Good riddance.

"I'm usually done by ten. You can come to my place."

"Perfect." Krista added the appointment to her calendar on her phone. "I'm texting you an invite."

Lacey stared. "What does that even mean?"

You would be so happy about this, Mom.

The peace she'd experienced in the tearoom flooded into the cracks of her heart, carrying a certainty that Mom had never judged Krista about her inadequacies as a caregiver and friend. No matter how large those things loomed in her mind.

Krista stepped to her sister's side and hugged her. "I'm so proud of you for going back to school, but you need to get in this century where there are things like digital calendars."

Lacey wrinkled her nose, as if she'd smelled something sour. "I can't afford a fancy phone. But I'm enjoying the college classes."

Krista thought of Jon's old phone. It would handle the scheduling and plenty of other automation. But instead of offering to give it to her sister, she asked, "How long does your program take?"

Lacey laughed ruefully. "Too long. Nine more months. And I need a better paying job now since my car needs service."

Krista tilted her head and studied Lacey. Asking for help would never be easy for either of them. She didn't want her sister to feel inadequate but as far as the car went, the solution was a no-brainer.

"Todd can look at it for you. You know he enjoys working on cars."

That was true. And he'd changed the oil and handled minor repairs on Lacey's car when she'd been married. Grant had worked too many extra shifts and claimed to be too tired after that to handle those things.

Lacey shook her head. Krista nudged her. "Please let him help."

Her sister swallowed a few times and ducked her head. Blonde tresses fluttered in an attempted escape from the headband protecting Lacey's ears from the wind and holding the short layers out of her face.

"Maybe Saturday when you come for lunch."

Krista's heart lurched, and a grin spilled over her face. "He'll be chomping at the bit to go home, trying to shortchange our visit."

"Or it will take him hours to fix the stupid thing, and you'll be dying to get away."

Krista doubted that. They had months of catching up to do.

"Do you have to work in the afternoon?"

Lacey shrugged. "Maybe. But I can schedule a long lunch." She put her back to the railing. "I'm going to sit with

Merci."

The ferry trip would take another hour, and Krista had hoped to spend more time strengthening the bridge between their hearts. But Merci would be leaving soon, and Krista knew Lacey wanted to grab these uninterrupted moments.

Krista ducked her chin and forced a smile. "I'm enjoying the fresh air. I'll join you two in a few minutes."

Lacey nodded and trudged away, narrowly dodging two boys chasing each other across the deck. Their squeals of glee sounded like hungry seagulls fighting for a crab leg.

Krista leaned into the railing and shook her head. When did their kids grow up? How was it possible Merci was moving to another state? She might be getting engaged soon.

Be at the center of that relationship, Lord. Give them wisdom.

Krista sighed, closed her eyes, and tilted her face toward the sun. Highlights from the week in Victoria replayed in her mind. Mom had exacted a promise from Merci to carry out the intervention Mom had planned. And, somehow, things had been worked out between all of them.

Help Merci realize her gifts, Lord. I trust you to show her the right path. Help Lacey do the same.

What about you? A voice whispered in the quiet place of her soul.

Goose bumps raced up her spine. Did God expect her to pray for her job? She'd been doing that for months, and the answer had been a resounding no. Besides, of all the transitions in life, hers was the smallest.

Although, she could make it bigger. She bit her lip and squinted over the vast expanse of water. Lacey was right. Krista didn't need to work for an income. She could afford to quit her communications job and be a substitute teacher. Wouldn't that experience look better on her resume when she applied for positions next school year?

Thanks for nudging me in the right direction, Lord.

Krista's cell phone rang, sounding the distinct tone for her husband. She swiped the screen and pressed the device to her ear. "Am I back in the US?"

She loved teasing him about stalking her with some application he'd activated on every family member's phone. His steadfast care sent warmth pooling low in her gut. And teasing was her husband's love language.

Todd chuckled. "I wasn't stalking you, so I don't know if you are. But I just got off an interesting call."

Krista stiffened. She meandered to a corner partially shielded from the wind. "Oh?"

"Mr. Anderson."

"The principal at City High?"

"That's the one."

Her heart skipped before tumbling toward her stomach. What would the principal want from her? It was too late for a new position to open, and she was tired of having her hopes for a classroom dashed.

She swallowed hard, managing to croak, "Okay."

"He had some concerning news. Mrs. Tindle had some complications, and her doctor put her on bed rest."

Mrs. Tindle was the language arts teacher Krista had agreed to sub for in January after her baby was born. Something flipped in Krista's chest. This wasn't good news.

"That's horrible. I hope the baby will be all right."

"Everything seems fine." He paused. "They want to meet with you Monday so Mrs. Tindle can go over the curriculum she'd planned for the year." Krista's brain spun and the fluttering behind her breastbone accelerated. "Apparently, she'd like you to cover her class, maybe until April as originally planned or maybe longer."

"At the start of school?" She held her breath.

"Looks like you'll have your own classroom after all, Kris."

The rest of the details blurred until they signed off with the usual love declarations. Krista hugged the phone against a heart trying to burst from her ribcage. What had just happened?

She needed to tell the others. Before she could take a step in that direction, the wind buffeted against her. The sense of another presence filled her throat until she couldn't breathe.

First, she needed to thank God. This wasn't the answer she'd longed for, but it wasn't a closed door.

Thank you for providing this job. Take care of Mrs. Tindle and her baby.

Something invisible held her in place. The wind ceased. In the calm, a rush of realization overwhelmed her.

Krista had been wrong for months. She hadn't been cursed for her prayer and emotional response the day Mom died. But she'd blamed God for her lack of a job. He didn't withhold forgiveness, but he had expected her to seek reconciliation with her sister. She'd had all manner of inaccurate thoughts about him.

Forgive me, Jesus. After knowing you all these years, I still don't know you.

Another thought struck her. She'd made things right with Lacey, and as soon as she'd released control over her job situation by deciding to quit the job she had, God had answered her larger prayer.

Tears filled her eyes. God amazed her.

With light steps, she hurried toward the table where her traveling companions waited. A balloon expanded in her chest, stopping her forward motion when she identified the wild sensation.

Hope.

With a smile, she slid into a chair on the sunny side of the table across from her niece. "You'll never guess what happened."

Two faces turned toward her, interest plain in their avid expressions.

Sunshine burst through her soul and beamed on her face. How glorious to have someone excited to share her good news.

This was the joy she expected when God answered her prayers.

She could hardly wait to get home and organize her classroom.

Her classroom.

Thank you, Lord. For all of it.

Especially for this trip her mother had planned. Their girls' trip had proved to be an antidote for the poison of secrets and misunderstandings.

And tell Mom thank you, too. Her plan worked its magic.

Angelic Intervention

In the garden alone
    So far from home
    Missing the one
    Who planned the fun
    Wishing and missing
    Missing and wishing
    A breeze stirs your hair
    Is someone there?
    Heaven's gates are closed they say
    Residents don't want to stray
    Maybe they swung open today
    You're sure she would find a way
    Fragrant roses
    Touching noses
    Busy bees
    On her knees
    You know that hat
    Your heart wants that
    Stranger to be
    Someone to see
    A message of peace
    A message of hope
    Missing and wishing
    Wishing and missing
    Her voice sounds so clear
    Each step brings her near
    That whisper you hear
    Brings so much cheer
    In the garden
    Not alone
    Among the roses
    Finding home

After Words

Although the idea behind these stories was inspired by an actual event, the characters are purely fictional. If they resemble my mother, sister, niece, and me, it's because every author draws on personal experience to add depth, reality, and relatability to their stories and characters.

Here's the true part. My mother made reservations for a trip to Victoria, BC. A trip she hoped the four of us would enjoy together. When that trip was canceled, my writer's brain wondered: what if the girls went on the trip anyway?

What you read here proves how a simple seed planted in the fertile imagination of a writer grows.

The characters you meet in the pages of this book have appeared in three iterations of a short story written November of 2014. It was part of a collection of short stories I wrote during the first National Novel Writing Month after my mother passed away. "Elephant in the Tearoom" gave me a place to acknowledge and address the grief her passing caused.

For writers, writing is the best therapy. Many therapists assign journaling activities because they understand writing can be cathartic, even for people who don't make up stories for a living.

That original short story resonated with me, and I decided to develop it into a novel written from three perspectives. This required a ton of additional planning, research about Vancouver Island, and many months to write a first draft. After getting approval from my sister and niece (since I suspected people who knew us and read the book would think it was about us), I began pitching the story to agents and editors.

While a few of them showed interest in the premise, all agreed 72,000 words didn't meet genre expectations. Contemporary women's fiction novels range between 80 to 100,000 words. One agent told me that if I could bring the word count to at least 80,000 words, he would look at it.

At the same writer's conference, I was pitching a proposal I had for a memoir/Bible study on grief. In fact, that was the only project I'd planned to pitch at the conference, but when free sessions opened, I jumped in to talk up *Elephant in the Tearoom*. In hindsight, I see that was God's way of confirming the story of those four women was a project of my heart.

The nonfiction proposal wasn't well-received.

The disappointment stung like rejection always does. And since I'd gotten no takers for my fiction either, it sounded like a door slamming in my face.

I let go of both projects.

Except I didn't.

A year passed. During a pitching event held bi-yearly on

Twitter, I tweeted the premise for the novel. An agent asked to read the manuscript. Not a few pages. The whole thing. A synopsis needed to accompany the manuscript, but she wanted to read the entire story.

My heart hoped that meant these characters would see the light of day from between the covers of a published book.

In the end, the way I'd written the story didn't mesh with what the agent had imagined from the pitch. Once again, it was shot down, and I easily shrugged off the second refusal. At the time, I was writing and publishing other stories.

But the characters kept whispering in my ear. Merci told me she had a whole story in California, and if I wrote about the trip to British Columbia, it would be a perfect teaser. Lacey emphasized that she wanted to move on. Could I please write her out of the dark place the first novel ended?

When I decided to write short stories and flash fiction for National Novel Writing Month in 2021, the first thing I wrote was the story of the mom making plans for the trip. You guessed it: the first story in this collection.

You know how that one ends.

And now you know how it began, too. Maybe you even understand the long, winding path it took to make it into your hands.

A quick note here about The Butchart Gardens. The rose garden isn't as described in this book. There is no feeble blue rose set apart from the others, and I saw no volunteers laboring among the bushes when I toured the beautiful grounds.

I took license on those things because they served my

story. I hope you'll forgive me for amending the reality of that lovely historical site so Lacey could find the peace she needed.

My deepest thanks to:

- God for calling and gifting me
- Jeff for believing I would write many stories
- Connie for being my biggest cheerleader
- Mom and Gram for modeling the strengths and graces of strong womanhood
- Two of my students for lending me their lovely names (Mercedes and Krista)
- My early readers for their insights
- Juli Sellers for the wise edits that made my vision a reality
- You for reading to the very last page.

Sharon Hughson

Meet Sharon Hughson

Sharon Hughson is called to share the truth through stories. Fiction shouldn't shy away from relating difficult circumstance, and she strives to present relatable characters handling even the ugliest situations in a realistic way that doesn't dishonor Christ. More importantly, she writes to encourage her readers.

As an avid and voracious reader, Sharon dives into books of nearly every genre and her writing of sweet romances, biblical fictionalizations, and Christian women's fiction reflect those loves. Since learning to read, she sought the escape offered in a well-told tale, but as she's grown older, she appreciates stories that reinforce her values the most.

A native Pacific Northwesterner, Sharon makes her home near the Columbia River in Oregon. When she's not writing or reading, Sharon coaches other writers, travels on adventures with her husband of three decades, and spoils her four grandchildren much to the chagrin of her cats.

See all her titles on her Amazon Author Page. To connect with Sharon, follow her on Facebook or Substack.

More from this author:

Romance
An Unexpected Homecoming
Mimi and the Banker

Biblical Fiction
Reflections: A Pondering Heart
Reflections: A Laboring Hand
Reflections: An Adoring Spirit